# THE USBORNE BOOK OF SCIENCE

This book contains the three titles, the **Usborne Introduction to Physics,** the **Usborne Introduction to Chemistry** and the **Usborne Introduction to Biology.**

# INTRODUCTION TO
# PHYSICS

## Amanda Kent and Alan Ward

### Consultant: Dr M. P. Hollins
### Designed by Iain Ashman
### Edited by Jenny Tyler
Computer program by John Freeman

Illustrated by Sue Stitt, Chris Lyon, Jeremy Gower, Simon Roulstone and Mick Gillah.

WITH COMPUTER PROGRAM LISTING

# Contents

Additional illustrations by Jim Bamber, Jeremy Banks,
Hayward & Martin, Rob McCaig, Elaine Mills,
Martin Newton, Graham Round, Graham Smith and
Ian Stephen. Additional designs by Glenn Lord
and Stanley Sweet.

First published in 1984 by
Usborne Publishing Ltd, 20 Garrick Street,
London WC2E 9BJ, England.

Copyright © 1984 Usborne Publishing.

Printed in Belgium

# What is physics?

Physics is to do with all the things around you and the energy they have. It is about why things get hot, what light is, how things move and make sounds, and so on.

It was the Ancient Greeks who first studied science and some of the ideas of physics come from them. Even the word

"physics" comes from an Ancient Greek word. Many of the basic laws and principles of physics are several hundred years old, but this doesn't mean they are old-fashioned or out of date. Most modern scientific discoveries are based on them and you need to know about them to understand how anything from a bicycle to a spaceship works.

The main areas of physics are light, heat, sound, mechanics, electricity and magnetism and this book has sections on each of these. There are experiments to help you understand some of the important ideas in physics. These are designed so that

you can find most of the things you need at home or in a nearby shop. If you find that an experiment doesn't work first time, don't worry – this often happens in science. The conditions may not be quite right and are interfering without you realizing. Just try again.

While reading this book, try and think about things around you and see how they fit in with the ideas you are reading about. You may think of your own experiments to do, too, to test the things you read about.

Towards the back of the book there is a physics computer program written to work on most common makes of home computer. If you have one of these or can borrow one from someone, type it in and try it out. It is all about using electricity in the home.

At the very back of the book are pages of physics words, where you can find definitions of some of the words you will meet in the book and the proper wording of some of the laws, such as Newton's Laws.

You will find answers to most of the questions and puzzles at the back of the book too. Some questions do not have answers; they are things for you to think about.

# All about energy

The world you live in is full of energy: light, heat, electricity and sound are some of the forms that energy takes. You use your own energy to move about and do your work. Most energy comes from the Sun, which provides heat and light for plants to grow, to keep you warm and let you see. Even fuels, such as oil and gas, were made from plants that absorbed the Sun's energy as they grew, millions of years ago.

## Potential and kinetic energy

Food you eat and petrol in a motorbike are forms of stored energy that can be used to make you or the motorbike move. These are both "potential energy" and they change to "kinetic energy" when things move.

## Chemical energy

Fuel in rockets and explosives in fireworks have potential chemical energy, changing to kinetic energy when rockets take off and fireworks explode.

## Gravitational energy

If you put something high up, you give it potential energy, which has come from your muscles. If it falls, its potential energy changes to kinetic energy.

## Strain energy

All solids, but especially springs and elastic, have this. The energy is potential when something is stretched or squeezed and changes to kinetic energy when let go.

**Chemical energy**

**Gravitational energy**

**Strain energy**

## Scare your friends

Find a piece of stiff card that fits into a long envelope which opens at one end. Cut a square in the card and loop a rubber band over the card. Put a small piece of card through the band and stick a piece of paper to each side of the card, trapping the rubber band.

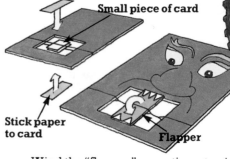

**Small piece of card**

**Stick paper to card**

**Flapper**

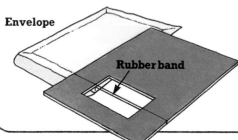

**Envelope**

**Rubber band**

Wind the "flapper" many times to give it potential energy. Put the card into the envelope and give it to your friends. When they pull the card out, potential energy changes to kinetic as the flapper starts to spin round.

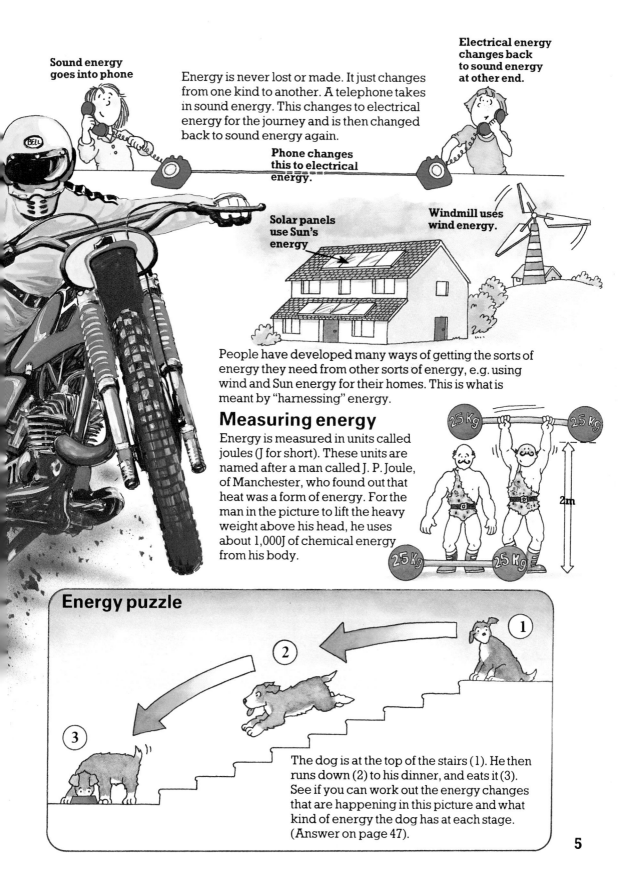

**Sound energy goes into phone**

Energy is never lost or made. It just changes from one kind to another. A telephone takes in sound energy. This changes to electrical energy for the journey and is then changed back to sound energy again.

**Phone changes this to electrical energy.**

**Electrical energy changes back to sound energy at other end.**

**Solar panels use Sun's energy**

**Windmill uses wind energy.**

People have developed many ways of getting the sorts of energy they need from other sorts of energy, e.g. using wind and Sun energy for their homes. This is what is meant by "harnessing" energy.

## Measuring energy

Energy is measured in units called joules (J for short). These units are named after a man called J. P. Joule, of Manchester, who found out that heat was a form of energy. For the man in the picture to lift the heavy weight above his head, he uses about 1,000J of chemical energy from his body.

25 Kg    25 Kg

2m

25 Kg    25 Kg

## Energy puzzle

The dog is at the top of the stairs (1). He then runs down (2) to his dinner, and eats it (3). See if you can work out the energy changes that are happening in this picture and what kind of energy the dog has at each stage. (Answer on page 47).

5

# Light energy

Nearly all the energy you need comes from the Sun; it is a source of light and heat energy. There are other sources of light, such as light bulbs, but most of the things you see do not give off light. Light coming from a source bounces off them, and some of that light goes into your eyes and makes you see them.

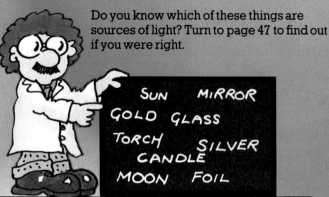

Do you know which of these things are sources of light? Turn to page 47 to find out if you were right.

SUN    MIRROR
GOLD  GLASS
TORCH      SILVER
   CANDLE
MOON   FOIL

## 1 How does light move?

Cork (and water) go up and down.

Energy travels in this direction.

Direction of light energy.

Up and down vibrations at right angles to wave's movement

If you try to see how light is actually travelling you will find it impossible. Physicists believe it travels in some ways like water, as a wave motion. They think light energy is carried along very tiny ripples, much smaller than water waves.

Imagine a cork on a pond. Waves make the cork bob up and down but it doesn't move in the direction the wave is going. Light waves vibrate similarly, up and down and also from side to side, while the light energy moves forward.

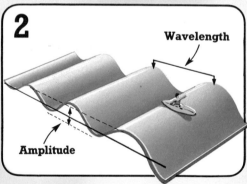

## 2

Wavelength

Amplitude

In order to compare waves, three measurements are taken: wavelength, which is the length from the top of one wave to the top of the next; amplitude, which is the height of the wave, and frequency, which is the number of waves that pass a certain point each second.

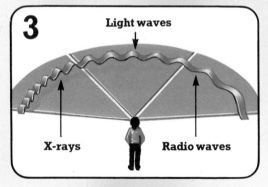

## 3

Light waves

X-rays          Radio waves

Light waves belong to a family of waves called the electromagnetic spectrum*. This includes X-rays, television, radio and heat waves. They all travel at the same speed, but their wavelengths are different and they have different effects on things.

**6**

*See page 40 for more about the electromagnetic spectrum.*

# Shadows

**Light bounces off mirror**

**Light goes through transparent things.**

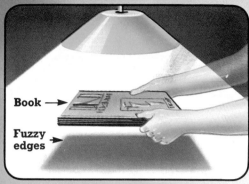

**Book** →

**Fuzzy edges** →

Some things, such as glass and air, allow light to pass straight through them, and are called transparent. When light hits something opaque (which means that the light waves are not able to pass through) a shadow is made where the light does not reach.

Hold a book under a light. You will see a shadow beneath it which has slightly fuzzy edges. Light waves hitting the book are bounced off. The shadow has fuzzy edges because the light bulb is large. Each point on the light bulb gives a sharp shadow, but in a slightly different place.

On a sunny day, see how long your shadow is at midday, and then late in the afternoon. The length of your shadow depends on the angle at which the light is hitting you. Try to think of

light as travelling as masses of tiny waves from a source. These waves move in straight lines until they hit something. Then they make a shadow where the light cannot reach.

## Shadows can be useful

You can make a sundial by cutting out a circle of white card, pushing a knitting needle through the centre and sticking the needle into the ground. Mark where the Sun's shadow falls each hour, and you have made a "clock".

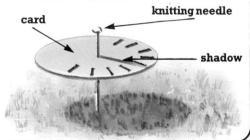

**knitting needle**

**card**

**shadow**

Shadows used to help people tell the time before clocks were invented. They used sundials. Some people still have them in their gardens. The time is "read" from the sundial, either by the length or the position of the shadow. It only works, of course, when the Sun is shining.

## How fast does light travel?
Light travels at an enormous speed. It covers 300 thousand kilometres in every second, which is more than 500 thousand times as fast as Concorde.

# Seeing things

Eyes and cameras work in the same way – light travels into them and makes images inside. If you make this "pinhole camera" you will see how this works.

**1** Find an old shoebox, make a hole 4 cm across in one end, cover it with black paper, sticking it down inside.

**2** Cut away most of the other end and cover this with greaseproof paper to make a screen. Put the lid on and stick it down with tape.

Screen

Light rays

**3** Make a pinhole through the black paper and put the box near to a light bulb. Look at the screen to see an upside down image of the light bulb.

Pinhole

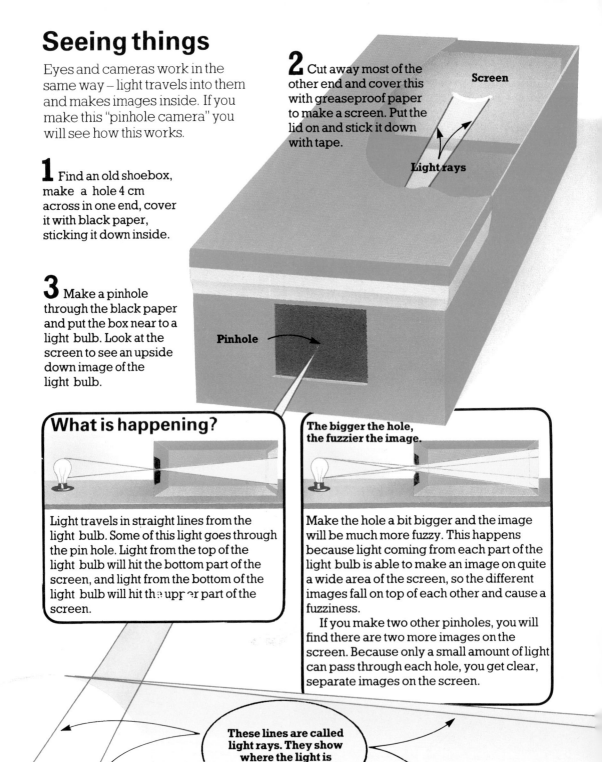

## What is happening?

Light travels in straight lines from the light bulb. Some of this light goes through the pin hole. Light from the top of the light bulb will hit the bottom part of the screen, and light from the bottom of the light bulb will hit the upper part of the screen.

### The bigger the hole, the fuzzier the image.

Make the hole a bit bigger and the image will be much more fuzzy. This happens because light coming from each part of the light bulb is able to make an image on quite a wide area of the screen, so the different images fall on top of each other and cause a fuzziness.

If you make two other pinholes, you will find there are two more images on the screen. Because only a small amount of light can pass through each hole, you get clear, separate images on the screen.

These lines are called light rays. They show where the light is going.

## Taking a photograph with the pinhole camera

To take a photograph, remove the greaseproof paper and find a well fitting back for the box. Under red light put some photographic paper in the back of the camera, and stick the camera back down well. Cover the pinhole with your finger.

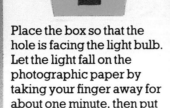

Place the box so that the hole is facing the light bulb. Let the light fall on the photographic paper by taking your finger away for about one minute, then put the box under red light again.

Remove the paper, move it around in a dish of "developer" until the picture appears. Dip it in water to wash it, put it into a dish of "fixer", and wash it again for 20 minutes.

## What lenses do

The photographs that can be taken with a pinhole camera are not very clear. This is because there is no lens in it. There are lenses in your eyes, in magnifying glasses, telescopes, microscopes and cameras. In all these, the lens bends the light so the light rays can all meet at a particular point. Lenses are always transparent, and they have curved edges.

Try on the glasses that some of your friends wear. You will discover that some are much stronger than others; the stronger glasses will make your eyes feel odder.

**Normal sight**

Retina

If your eyes are working properly, the light rays coming from a point meet at a point on the retina, which is at the back of your eye.

**Shortsighted**

Retina

If you are shortsighted, the rays come together in front of the retina. You need lenses that curve inwards, called concave lenses, to correct this.

**Longsighted**

Retina

If you are longsighted, the light rays come together behind the retina. You need glasses with lenses that curve outwards, called convex lenses, to correct this.

Eyes and cameras make images in the same way as a pinhole camera.

**Iris – this can close up to let less light pass, depending on how bright it is outside.**

**Receptive area – this is where the light ends up, it has special chemicals that react to the light. (The camera film has special chemicals too.)**

**Pupil – this is the hole that lets in light, like the pinhole.**

**Lens – this helps to bend light so it all arrives at the same point on the retina, at the back of the eye (or the film in a camera).**

9

# Reflection

Lots of things around you reflect light: windows, glasses, cars that have been well polished, shiny boots, a pool of still water, silver foil. But reflection is best in mirrors, because they are so smooth and shiny.

Stand next to a friend in front of a mirror. Can you see how they look different from how you normally see them? This is because the mirror changes everything around. Try winking your right eye, and it seems that your left eye is winking back at you in the mirror. What you see in the mirror is a "wrong-way-round" image of yourself.

## The law of reflection

If you throw a ball straight at a wall, it will bounce straight back. If you throw it at an angle it will bounce off at the same angle. Try it yourself and see. This is the law of reflection, and it works for light too.

Draw two lines at equal angles to a flat mirror. Shine a ray of light (you could use a torch) along one of these lines. You will see that the mirror reflects the ray along the other line. The ray and its reflection will always make the same angle with the mirror.

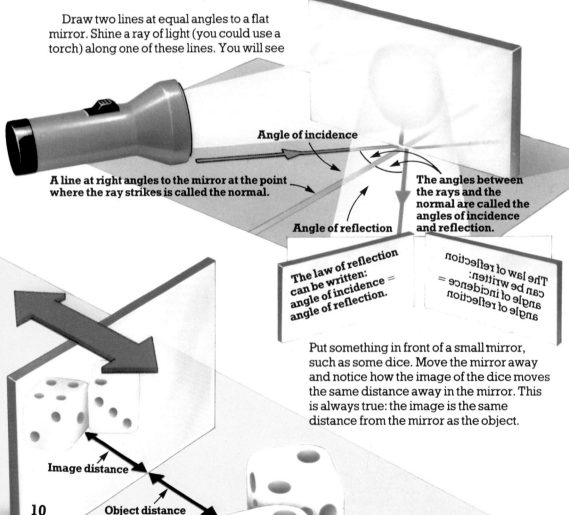

**Angle of incidence**

**A line at right angles to the mirror at the point where the ray strikes is called the normal.**

**Angle of reflection**

**The angles between the rays and the normal are called the angles of incidence and reflection.**

The law of reflection can be written: angle of incidence = angle of reflection.

The law of reflection can be written: angle of incidence = angle of reflection.

Put something in front of a small mirror, such as some dice. Move the mirror away and notice how the image of the dice moves the same distance away in the mirror. This is always true: the image is the same distance from the mirror as the object.

**Image distance**

**Object distance**

# Refraction

Light waves can travel through transparent things, but they slow down when they enter them. It is rather like when you walk into the sea; the water slows you down. Light travels fastest in air, 25% slower in water and 35% slower in glass.

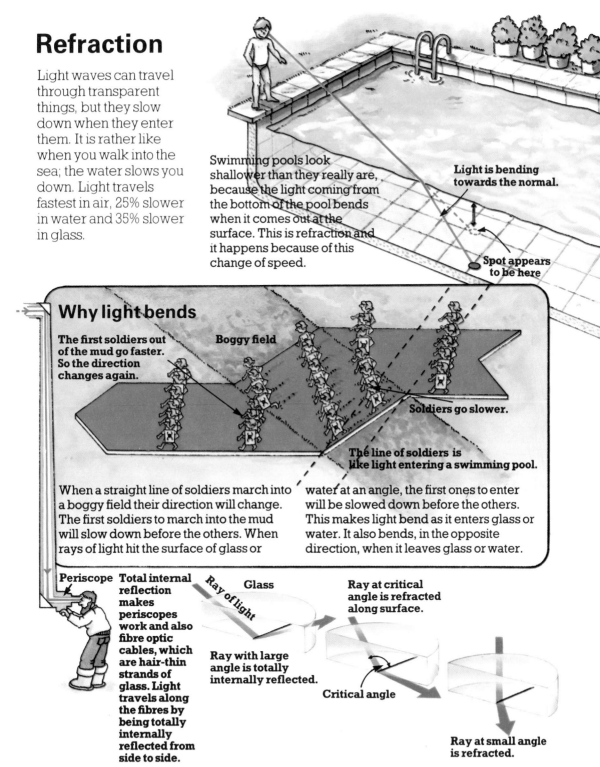

Swimming pools look shallower than they really are, because the light coming from the bottom of the pool bends when it comes out at the surface. This is refraction and it happens because of this change of speed.

**Light is bending towards the normal.**

**Spot appears to be here**

## Why light bends

**The first soldiers out of the mud go faster. So the direction changes again.**

**Boggy field**

**Soldiers go slower.**

**The line of soldiers is like light entering a swimming pool.**

When a straight line of soldiers march into a boggy field their direction will change. The first soldiers to march into the mud will slow down before the others. When rays of light hit the surface of glass or water at an angle, the first ones to enter will be slowed down before the others. This makes light bend as it enters glass or water. It also bends, in the opposite direction, when it leaves glass or water.

**Periscope** **Total internal reflection makes periscopes work and also fibre optic cables, which are hair-thin strands of glass. Light travels along the fibres by being totally internally reflected from side to side.**

**Ray of light** **Glass**

**Ray at critical angle is refracted along surface.**

**Ray with large angle is totally internally reflected.**

**Critical angle**

**Ray at small angle is refracted.**

Sometimes, light can't get out of water or glass because it is hitting the surface at a very big angle. The light bounces back into the water or glass. This is called "total internal reflection" and it can be very useful.

Light sometimes comes out of the glass or water, but travels along the surface. It only does this when it hits the surface at a particular angle called the "critical angle". This angle is different for glass and water.

# Colour

Ordinary white light is a small group of waves in the electromagnetic spectrum.* It is a mixture of different colours, and each colour has a different wavelength**

Isaac Newton discovered that light is made up of different colours in 1666. He let a beam of sunlight coming through a hole in his window blind pass through a glass prism. (This is a triangular chunk of glass.) The prism split the light up into a band of colours on his wall. He called the band of colours the "solar spectrum".

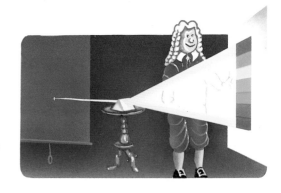

## Make a spectrum

When a ray of sunlight enters a raindrop, some of it is reflected back out. It is split into different colours because the raindrop acts as a prism, and a rainbow may be formed. On a bright sunny day you could try making a spectrum on the wall using the same principle. Position a mirror inside a plastic box filled with water. Put it opposite a window facing the Sun. The wedge of water between the surface and the mirror acts as a prism.

The wedge of water bends each different wavelength by a slightly different amount. Red has the longest wavelength and is bent the least. Violet has the shortest and is bent the most. The colours always appear in the same order: red, orange, yellow, green, blue, indigo, violet. (Remember, ROY-G-BIV.)

**If your wall is not white, tape or hold a sheet of paper over the place where the colours will appear.**

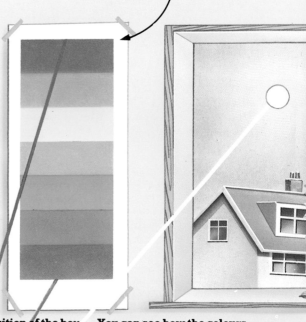

**Juggle the position of the box and the slant of the mirror, until you get a solar spectrum on the wall.**

**Water**

**Plastic box**

**Mirror**

**You can see how the colours mix to make white light by waggling your fingers in the water. The colours blur and become white.**

Although we say the spectrum is made up of the colours red, orange, yellow, green, blue, indigo and violet, each of these really consists of a whole range of wavelengths. The yellow band is lots of different yellows, for example, ranging from orangey yellows to greeny yellows.

*See page 40 for more about this.

**See page 6 for more about wavelengths.

# Colour mixing

You can mix colours in two ways: either by mixing different coloured lights together or by mixing up paints.

The three main coloured lights are red, green and blue. These are the three primary colours in science. If red, green and blue lights are mixed together they make white light, as is shown on the right.

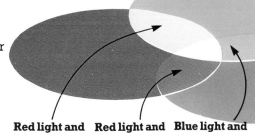

**Red light and green light mix to make yellow.**

**Red light and blue light mix to make magenta.**

**Blue light and green light mix to make cyan.**

Colour television pictures are made up from these three primary colours. The picture consists of thousands of tiny glowing dots, some red, some blue and some green. The light from the glowing dots mixes to form all the different colours you see on the screen.

Paints and all coloured things contain pigments. When we say something is coloured red, it is because the pigments are absorbing all the colours in the light that is hitting it except the red, which is reflected. A blue object has pigments that absorb all the colours in white light except blue.

**Red light**

## Why leaves are green

The chemical processes that go on in plants need mainly red light. As long as a plant is alive, the red light from sunlight is absorbed by a pigment called chlorophyll inside the leaves and stems. The remaining light, mostly green, is reflected, giving plants their greeny colour.

## Make a colour mixer

Cut out a circle of card, about 8cm across. Draw seven equal-sized segments on it and colour them in the colours of the rainbow. Make a hole in the middle and stick a pencil through it, point downwards. Try spinning your top. What colour is it when it is spinning fast? Why do you think this is?

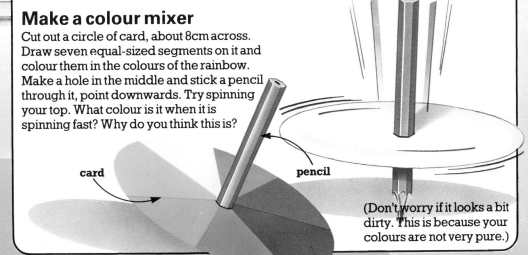

**card**

**pencil**

(Don't worry if it looks a bit dirty. This is because your colours are not very pure.)

# Heat energy

Heat is another form of energy and is also measured in joules. The hotter something is, the more heat energy it contains. If two objects are put in contact, heat will flow from the warmer into the cooler object. Heat can also be transferred by electromagnetic radiation*. Other forms of energy can be converted into heat: in a lamp, for example, electrical energy is converted into both light and heat.

## What does heat do?

Absolutely everything around you is made of particles called atoms which are much too tiny to see. They are usually joined into little groups called molecules. These vibrate backwards, forwards and sideways all the time with kinetic energy. They even vibrate in solids, though not enough to lose their places in a neat pattern. When heat waves hit the molecules, the energy of the waves changes to kinetic energy which makes the molecules move around even more. The molecules knock against each other, rather like marbles hitting one another, and the vibration energy is passed on from one to another.

## See how molecules move

Put some peas in a jar and shake the jar very gently. The peas will vibrate, but will stay in roughly the same places. This is what happens when a solid is heated. Shaking the jar more will give the peas more energy. They will roll over each other like the molecules in a liquid. If you shake harder some of the peas may even jump out of the jar. This is what happens when a liquid boils: some of the molecules jump out and make a gas.

14

*There is more about heat radiation on pages 16 and 40.

Here you can see what happens when water changes its "state", that is, changes from solid to liquid to gas.

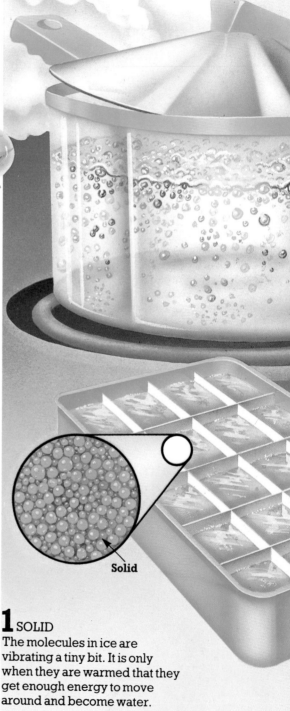

**Solid**

**1** SOLID
The molecules in ice are vibrating a tiny bit. It is only when they are warmed that they get enough energy to move around and become water.

**Gas**

## 3 GAS

Steam takes up more space than water, which is why it tries to push up the saucepan lid. Steam, which is gas, contains molecules that are flying around in the air. If they hit something cold they will change back to water again. They pass their energy to the cooler surface, which, as a result, is warmed up slightly.

## 2 LIQUID

As water gets hotter and hotter, the molecules have more and more energy and are able to move further and faster. Some soon have enough energy to jump out of the liquid. When the water is boiling, lots of the molecules have enough kinetic energy to leave the water as steam.

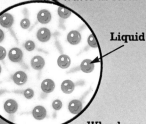

**Liquid**

**Why do you think a saucepan boils over sometimes?**

### Water is odd

In most substances, the liquid takes up more space than the solid because the molecules move further apart. Water is odd because when a lump of ice melts, the water that is left occupies *less* space. This happens because of the way the molecules are arranged in ice. Pipes sometimes burst in winter because freezing water expands and cracks them.

## Can you tell how hot something is?

Don't use boiling water!

COLD  WARM  HOT

Your body is not very good at this. Fill three bowls with water, one with hot, one with cold and the other with warm water. Put one hand in the hot water, and the other in cold water for a few seconds. Then put them both in the warm water and your hands tell you different things. The one that was in hot water will think the warm water is very cold and the one that was in cold water will find it hot.

Temperature is the measurement of how hot something is and, as we cannot measure it ourselves, we need something to do it for us. Thermometers, such as the special medical one below, are used for this.

**Narrow part –** this gives you time to read the thermometer because once the mercury has passed this point it can't go down again until the thermometer is shaken.

**Bulb – full of liquid mercury.** When the surroundings get hotter, its molecules move around more and the liquid expands up the tube.

**Scale of temperature –** this shows the temperature of the surroundings measured in degrees Celsius. 0°C is the temperature of ice and 100°C the temperature of boiling water. Our body temperature does not vary much from 37°C so this thermometer only goes from 35°C to 42°C.

There are several other kinds of thermometers. Some use a special sort of alcohol to measure very low temperatures, others work by using gas. Temperature can even be measured using electricity.

# How does heat travel?

Heat energy can travel in waves in the same way as light. This is called heat radiation. Heat waves travel from the Sun at 300 million metres (about eight times round the Earth) per second, to reach us across about 240 million kilometres of empty space. The journey takes about eight minutes. The more "red hot" something gets the more heat it radiates. Electric fires, hot plates and light bulbs all radiate heat.

The heat waves themselves are not hot, but when they are stopped and absorbed by something, that thing will get hot. Dark-coloured things absorb more radiant heat than light things. If a swimming pool is solar-heated, black panels are used. Water from the pool circulates under the panels and gets warm because the panels absorb the Sun's heat well.

Radiant heat is reflected by white and shiny surfaces. People tend to wear pale colours in summer because the heat is reflected off them. In hot countries, such as Australia, many of the cars are white. Try touching light and dark coloured cars when they have been in the hot sunshine. The dark ones are much hotter.

## Rising heat

As liquids and gases get warmer, their molecules have more kinetic energy and so can move further apart. They are now less "dense"* and each bit is lighter, so they can rise up. Cold liquid or gas, being more dense, sinks down. When heat is carried by liquids and gases in this way it is called convection.

**Gliders use convection currents.**

## How radiators work

Central heating radiators give off most of their heat by convection, not radiation. They warm the air around them which rises as convection currents. The cold air sinks and is warmed in turn.

*See page 25 to find out more about density.

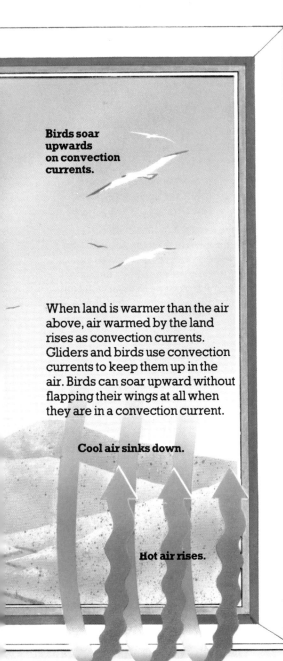

Birds soar upwards on convection currents.

When land is warmer than the air above, air warmed by the land rises as convection currents. Gliders and birds use convection currents to keep them up in the air. Birds can soar upward without flapping their wings at all when they are in a convection current.

**Cool air sinks down.**

**Hot air rises.**

Houses need to be well ventilated and air must circulate round the rooms. As air is warmed by heaters and fires, it becomes less dense, rises towards the ceiling, where it is mixed with cool air coming in the windows. It then sinks again.

# Invisible heat movement

Heat can actually move through some things without you knowing it is happening. It does this by movements of molecules. When molecules are heated they have more kinetic energy which they pass on by bumping against each other. When heat moves this way it is called conduction.

Some things are better at conducting heat than others. Air is a very bad conductor, and so are most clothes. In cold weather people wear woollen sweaters. The warmth of their bodies can only escape very slowly. In hot countries people wear very loose cotton clothes. The heat outside is not conducted towards their bodies because of the air between their skin and their clothes. Convection currents inside the clothes take the hot air away.

# Spoon test

Which spoon do you think will get hottest? The butter melts quickest on the silver spoon. Silver is the best conductor of heat here. The plastic spoon will get least hot. It is a bad conductor of heat, which is why saucepans often have plastic handles. Substances that are poor conductors of heat are called insulators.

Plastic  Silver  Wood

Butter  Peas  Steel  Hot water

You could try this yourself

Try any spoons you have.

# Puzzle
How is your home kept warm? Do you have radiators, open fires, gas fires, double glazing? Are you kept warm by radiation, conduction or convection? Or by all three?

# Sounds and noises

Sound is another form of energy. All sounds happen because something is vibrating, which makes molecules in the air begin to vibrate too. The molecules themselves are not the sound, but without them there is silence.

## What happens when you make a sound?

Try this with your ruler . . .

**Bend up and let go . . .**

Book

Ruler

1. When the ruler is up, air molecules are squashed together above the ruler and thinned out underneath.

2. When the ruler is down, molecules are crowded together underneath and thinned out above.

3. Meanwhile, the first group of close-together molecules is now expanding and pushing the next group of molecules above it together. The vibrating ruler is pushing the air into a pattern of molecules that are at first close together, then far apart.

## How you hear sound

You hear a humming noise because the pattern of molecules moving through the air hits your eardrum and makes it vibrate too. These vibrations trigger off tiny pulses of electricity which travel along nerves to your brain. Your brain interprets these pulses as sound.

Sounds can only travel if there are molecules around. In space there are no molecules so astronauts have to talk to each other by radio. (Radio waves, like light waves, can travel where there are no molecules.)

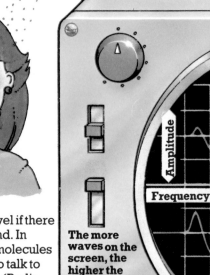

Amplitude

Frequency

**The more waves on the screen, the higher the frequency, and the higher the pitch of sound. Things that vibrate fast have a higher pitch.**

## How fast does sound travel?

Sound travels much faster through solids and liquids than through air. On land, an explosion at sea often sounds like two booms – sound waves travelling through the water and air arrive at different times.

Sound travels better through solids and liquids than through air. That's why American Indians used to put their ears to the ground to listen for horses.

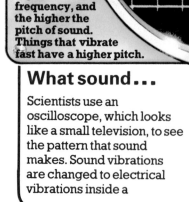

## What sound . . .

Scientists use an oscilloscope, which looks like a small television, to see the pattern that sound makes. Sound vibrations are changed to electrical vibrations inside a

## Underwater sounds

By sending out sound pulses, ships can detect whether something such as a submarine is below them in the water and how deep it is. The sound pulses are reflected back to the ship when they hit something. This is called sonar. Sound travels four times as fast in water as in air.

## Resonance

If you "ping" a glass with your finger, it will vibrate and ring. It does so with its own special frequency, called its natural frequency. A singer, singing a note of the same frequency, is supposed to be able to make a glass vibrate so much that it cracks. This is called resonance.

## Noises

Noises, such as heavy traffic, are made up of a jumble of vibrations of different frequencies. Their vibrations do not follow a regular pattern as those of other sounds do. The loudness of sounds and noises can be measured in decibels (dB). Very high decibel counts can damage people's ears and may cause deafness. Here you can see how loud some everyday sounds are.

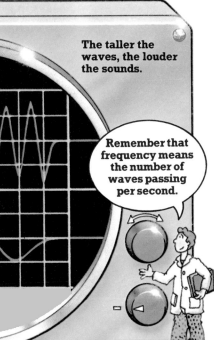

**The taller the waves, the louder the sounds.**

**Remember that frequency means the number of waves passing per second.**

## ...looks like

microphone and these are used to make wave shapes appear on the screen. The crests show where a big group of molecules is hitting the microphone.

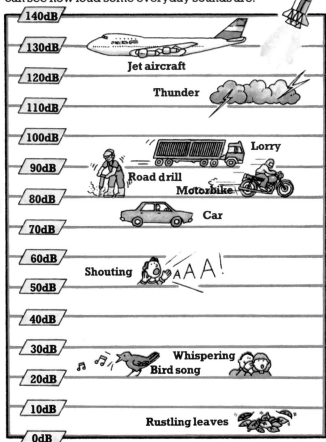

| | |
|---|---|
| 140dB | |
| 130dB | Jet aircraft |
| 120dB | |
| 110dB | Thunder |
| 100dB | |
| 90dB | Lorry |
| 80dB | Road drill / Motorbike |
| 70dB | Car |
| 60dB | |
| 50dB | Shouting AAA! |
| 40dB | |
| 30dB | Whispering |
| 20dB | Bird song |
| 10dB | |
| 0dB | Rustling leaves |

19

# Music

There are three main types of musical instrument, and in each one the notes that can be produced depend on what is vibrating.

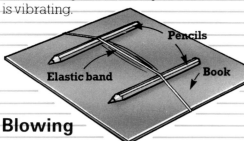

Elastic band · Pencils · Book

## Blowing

All wind instruments work by making a column of air vibrate. The pitch of the notes can be varied by changing the length of the air column. Try blowing across the tops of bottles containing water.

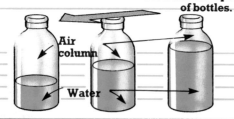

Blow across tops of bottles.

Air column · Water

## Plucking strings

When the strings of a guitar are plucked they vibrate and the air around them starts to vibrate too. If you put your fingers on the string you shorten the length of the bit that can vibrate, and this makes the pitch higher. Making strings tighter or using lighter strings also raises the pitch. Try stretching an elastic band around a book and two pencils. Change the vibrating length of the elastic band by moving the pencils closer together or farther apart.

Plastic · Rice · Elastic band · Bowl

## Tapping and hitting

Stretch some plastic tightly across the top of a bowl. Put some sugar or rice on the plastic, tap the top and see how the grains vibrate. Drums make "sounds" because their covering vibrates, sending sound waves into the air.

## Music puzzle

Can you think how all these things produce music – by blowing, plucking strings, or hitting? (Answers on page 47.)

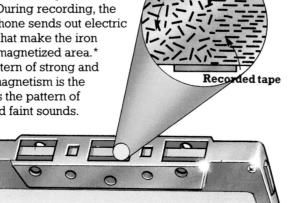

## How music is stored

Cassette tapes store sound as magnetism in a layer of iron oxide. During recording, the microphone sends out electric pulses that make the iron form a magnetized area.* The pattern of strong and weak magnetism is the same as the pattern of loud and faint sounds.

Iron oxide particles · Blank tape · Recorded tape

To make a record, the message on a "master tape" is converted back to electric pulses, which are fed to a "cutting head". This has a very sharp diamond point. It vibrates with the electric pulses and cuts grooves into a soft plastic disc. Loud sounds make the groove deeper and high notes make it more wavy. This plastic disc is used as a sort of mould. The records you buy are made from imprints of it.

*Magnets are explained on page 36.

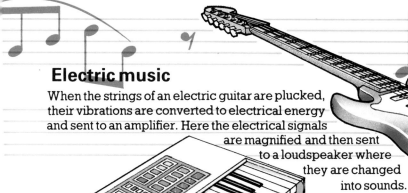

## Electric music

When the strings of an electric guitar are plucked, their vibrations are converted to electrical energy and sent to an amplifier. Here the electrical signals are magnified and then sent to a loudspeaker where they are changed into sounds.

## Synthesizers

Synthesizers make music by using electric signals instead of vibrations. They are usually connected to a keyboard. Each note played on the keyboard sends a particular electric message to the synthesizer. This then sets up an electrical code for the sound that is wanted. The code is sent to an amplifier and then a loudspeaker, which converts it to vibrations in the air that you can hear.

## Computer music

Several microcomputers have a tiny synthesizer inside the keyboard, which enables them to play simple tunes and make sounds. You have to type in a command such as "sound" or "ping" followed by the note you want and how long you want it played for.

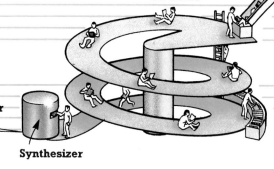

**Instructions from the micro**

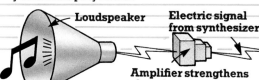

Loudspeaker

**Electric signal from synthesizer**

**Amplifier strengthens electrical signal.**

**Synthesizer**

## Compact discs

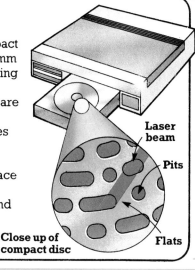

A very modern way of storing sound is on compact disc. These are only 120mm wide (a normal long playing record is 300mm wide). Instead of grooves there are millions of microscopic "pits and flats". Turntables for the discs have a laser beam instead of a stylus. The beam scans the surface of the disc, "reading" the pattern of pits and flats and converting this into electrical signals and then vibrations.

Laser beam

Pits

Flats

**Close up of compact disc**

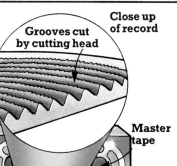

**Grooves cut by cutting head**

**Close up of record**

**Master tape**

21

# Mechanics

Mechanics is not just about garages. It is about everything that is happening to things – how heavy they are, what is pushing and pulling them, how they move and what they can do. The next ten pages are all about mechanics.

**Pulling 30N**

**Pushing 30N**

**Lifting 1000N**

**Squashing 20N**

## Forces

We are always pulling, pushing and lifting. A push or a pull is called a force. A force can get an object moving, or stop it from moving, or change the direction of its movement, or squeeze it and change its shape.

Force is measured in newtons (N), after a very famous scientist, Sir Isaac Newton (1642-1727). A force of one newton is quite a small force. The picture on the left shows people exerting forces and gives a rough idea of the size of these forces.

## Gravity

Newton's name is connected with the study of the force of gravitation – the pull we usually call gravity. He is said to have begun wondering about this pull when he saw an apple fall. There is a force between all objects that pulls them together. Usually this force is small, but the Earth is so big it has a strong pull. It pulls things like the apple towards it by the force of gravity.

The Moon is much smaller than Earth, and its gravitational pull is only one sixth of the pull of Earth's gravity. On the Moon you could kick a ball six times as far, and jump six times as high.

## How heavy are you?

Kilograms measure your mass, the "amount of stuff" inside you. The easiest way of finding out the mass of something is to measure its weight. Weight is the pull of gravity on an object, and is given in newtons because it is a force. To convert the mass into the weight, multiply it by the pull of the Earth (about 10 units) and give the answer in newtons. So if your mass is 60 kilograms (60kg for short), your weight is about 600N. When you stand on scales, the pointer is really showing your weight, but the scale is marked to show your mass directly, so it says 60kg, not 600N.

How much would you weigh on the Moon? And what would your mass be? Don't forget, the pull of the Moon is only 1/6 that of the Earth. (Answer on page 47.)

**Your weight = your mass x pull of the Earth.**

# Centre of gravity

The Earth's gravity pulls down on every single particle with a force equal to the weight of that particle. In a body, the forces seem to be concentrated at the "centre of gravity". Once the centre of gravity is hanging outside the base of the object, it will fall over.

**Boat falls over because its centre of gravity has moved "outside" its base.**

You put your arms out when you are trying to balance. By holding them out and moving them up and down, you are able to alter your centre of gravity so that it is still over your base (your feet) and you don't fall over. Why do you think a tight rope walker uses a pole?

## Stability

It is difficult to make something fall over if it is stable. Stable things have very low centres of gravity. Racing cars are built very low on the ground with a low centre of gravity so they can keep upright when cornering fast. Perhaps you can think of other stable things.

An empty plastic bottle is not very stable. You can knock it over easily because its centre of gravity is high. If some water is added, the weight in the bottom of the bottle makes the centre of gravity lower and it is now more stable. If the bottle is full of water, the centre of gravity is higher and it is not very stable again.

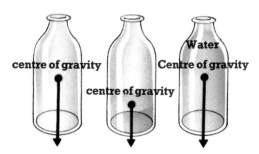

centre of gravity

centre of gravity

Water
Centre of gravity

# What is pressure?

Pressure is how much push there is on a certain area. Atmospheric pressure, for example, is measured by working out the weight of the air in newtons pressing down on a square metre of ground. It is given in newtons per square metre ($N/m^2$) and at sea level atmospheric pressure is $100,000 N/m^2$.

Anything, solid, liquid or gas, can exert pressure. The pull of gravity makes you push on the ground – through the area of your shoes that are touching the ground's surface. When a doctor measures your blood pressure, he measures how much the blood is being forced along your arteries and veins. Try

**Area is measured in square metres and pressure is measured in newtons per square metre ($N/m^2$).**

pushing your thumb into a piece of wood. You probably won't make a mark, but if you pushed with the same force on the top of a drawing-pin, you would be able to push deep into the wood. Your push is now concentrated over the much tinier area of the point.

## Crush a bottle

This experiment shows air pressure at work. Find an empty flimsy plastic bottle - the kind used for lemonade, cola or orange. Remove the cap.

**1** Put 2-3cm of hot water from the kitchen tap into the bottle. Quickly replace the cap and screw it down tightly.

**2** As the water cools, air inside the bottle cools and contracts and its pressure is reduced. The greater force of atmospheric pressure outside the bottle causes it to crush.

# Liquids can push too

Water and all liquids take the shape of whatever container they are in. All the time they are pressing outwards on the inside of the container, trying to escape.

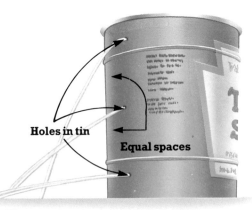

## Pressure experiment

Make three holes the same distance apart up the side of a tall tin, cover the holes with a strip of sticky tape and fill the tin with water. Stand it so its holes are next to a sink and pull off the tape. Water spurts out further from the lower holes because it is pressed out with a stronger push. This pressure is caused by the weight of water that lies above. So the deeper the water, the greater the pressure. (Try a taller tin and check this for yourself).

**Holes in tin**

**Equal spaces**

## Surface tension

Water molecules attracting each other.

**Pond skater**

Molecules in liquids attract each other and pull towards each other in all directions. The molecules at the surface, though, have nothing above them to attract, so they pull together much more on each side. This makes the surface layer act rather like a light skin. This is called surface tension. This skin is really quite strong. Some insects, such as the pond skater, can run across the surface of water.

## See surface tension happen

Arrange some matches on water in a bowl. If the surface in the centre is touched with blotting paper the matches move towards the centre. Blotting paper soaks up some of the water and the whole surface of the water including the matches is pulled towards the centre. If you touch the centre with a piece of soap the matches move away.

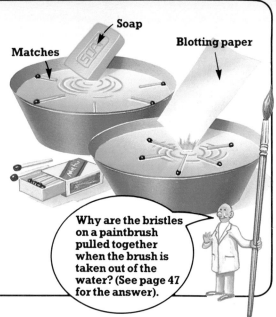

**Soap**

**Matches**

**Blotting paper**

## What is happening?

Some of the soap molecules dissolve in the water in the centre and the soap and water molecules mix. The pulling forces between water molecules break down, which means the surface tension is reduced and the water is pulled back from the centre by stronger forces on the edges.

Why are the bristles on a paintbrush pulled together when the brush is taken out of the water? (See page 47 for the answer).

## Why do we use soap?

Water molecules are more strongly attracted to each other than to other things. When soap is added the special "wetting agent" it contains breaks down the surface tension of the water molecules, which means they can wet things better.

# Bubbles

Bubbles are like elastic envelopes made from layers of soap or washing-up liquid and water. The air inside is slightly compressed and is pushing out from the centre equally in all directions. The liquid has two surfaces, both of which are pulling inwards in all directions.

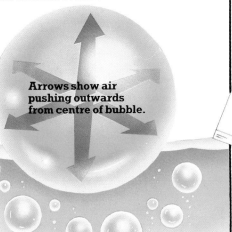

Arrows show air pushing outwards from centre of bubble.

# How does a steel ship float?

Steel has a much higher relative density than water, yet a steel ship can float. Look at the plan of a ship. It is not a solid lump of steel. There are lots of empty rooms full of air. Its *average* density is less than water. People can float in water, so our *average* density must be less than water too.

Plan of ship

# Displacement

When things float, the weight of water they push to the side (displace) is equal to their weight. You float better and displace less water when you breathe in. This is because having air in your lungs makes your average density less. Why do you think submarines take water into special tanks when they want to dive deep under the sea?

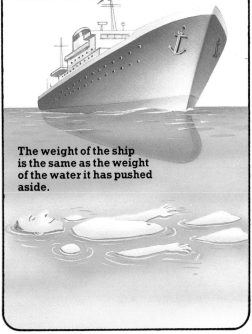

The weight of the ship is the same as the weight of the water it has pushed aside.

# Why do things float?

Whether something floats depends on how heavy it is compared to its volume. This is called its density. Scientists say that the density of water is 1, and then compare the densities of everything else to it. Only if its "relative density" is less than 1, can something float in water. Here are some relative densities.

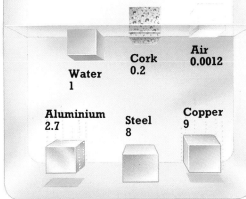

Water 1

Cork 0.2

Air 0.0012

Aluminium 2.7

Steel 8

Copper 9

# Stopping and going

Over 300 years ago Isaac Newton worked out a set of rules that explain the way in which things move. These rules can apply to anything, even the most modern machinery. You can see below that the way a pair of roller skates moves is to do with Newton's laws. As you read through these two pages, try and think of other things, like cars and trains, and how they move.

## Starting off

1. To make anything start moving, go faster or stop, a force is needed. This person needs a force (a push from his friend) to start him sliding across the ice on a tray.

**Push (force) needed to start moving**

2. Once moving, the person would carry on for ever at the same speed in a straight line unless a force acted upon him. This is Newton's first law*. Friction is important here – friction is a force that happens when two things rub together, such as the tray rubbing against the ice. Friction opposes motion and makes things slow down.

**Once moving a force is needed to stop things. (Friction is often the force that does this.)**

3. The person accelerates slowly up to a certain speed and also takes a little time to decelerate again. The time taken to change speed (accelerate or decelerate) depends on the size of the person. A bigger person would take longer. This resistance to change of movement is called "inertia". The bigger the person the more inertia he has.

## Quicker and faster

Newton found that things speed up (accelerate) quicker if the force pushing is greater. The person will accelerate faster across the ice if his friend pushes harder. If the person had less mass, the same force would accelerate him further. This is Newton's second law* of motion.

## Forwards and backwards, up and down

Whenever there is a force on one thing in one direction, another force is acting on something else in the opposite direction. This is Newton's third law.* When a gun is fired, at the same time that the bullet shoots out of the barrel, the gun kicks back into your shoulder. Somebody pushing a person across the ice on a tray will find themselves falling backwards as the person on the tray sets off forwards.

*See page 46 for the exact wording of Newton's laws of motion.

## Friction can be helpful

When you skate on ice, your skates move easily. There is very little friction between your skates and the ice because the ice is smooth and your skates are sharp. But on roads you need to grip the surface in order to walk. You need friction. Roads are not smooth and shoes and tyres are made with ridges on them to make more friction between them and the road.

**Tread on tyres increases friction.**

## Friction in liquids

There is friction between the layers of molecules in some liquids such as treacle, honey and oil, which is why they are sticky and slow to pour. They are called viscous liquids; and some of them, such as oil, can be very useful for stopping two pieces of metal in a machine rubbing together. Oil is put between the metals so that instead of lots of friction between the pieces of metal there is only the small amount of friction in the oil.

Why do you think we don't use water to reduce friction?

**Oil reduces friction.**

## Liquid inertia

Liquids have inertia too. You can use this fact to tell the difference between a hardboiled egg and a raw egg. Spin them both on separate saucers. Stop them with your fingers, then let go almost immediately. The raw egg starts spinning again. This is because the layers of liquid inside the raw egg are still spinning round with "moving inertia".

## Roller skates

Here you can see how Newton's laws of motion affect roller skating.

**The skater's muscles produce the force that he needs to push against the air resistance, to go uphill or to accelerate. Once he is moving, if there were no forces acting such as air resistance and friction, he would carry on for ever (Newton's first law).***

**The skater gets going by pushing backwards against the ground. The ground pushes him forward (Newton's 3rd law)* and he starts moving.**

**The harder he pushes, the faster he will accelerate (Newton's 2nd law).***

**Bigger people take longer to build up speed.**

**Greasing wheels reduces friction.**

# Speed, acceleration and gravity

Speed is how fast you are going. It is the distance you travel in a certain time. Velocity is different from speed. It is a measure of how fast you are going in a particular direction. Both speed and velocity are measured in metres per second (m/s) or more commonly kilometres per hour (km/h). When you change velocity you either go faster (accelerate), slower (decelerate) or change direction. Acceleration and deceleration are both measured in metres per second per second ($m/s^2$), because you are changing velocity with time.

## Slower and faster experiment

This plane is accelerating (increasing speed) as it takes off.

It decelerates (decreases its speed) as it lands.

Friction helps make planes decelerate. You can see friction working by doing this experiment. Tape a paper clip to the side of a jar and roll it along a hard floor. The clicking sound of the clip will get slower and slower. Friction between the jar and the ground makes the jar decelerate. The air around the jar is also in the way, and this is called air resistance.

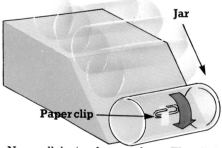

Jar

Paper clip

Now roll the jar down a slope. The clicks get quicker. The jar is being accelerated by the force of gravity pulling it downwards. Physicists have found that gravity always pulls things on Earth with the same acceleration – the acceleration due to gravity, which is $9.8\,m/s^2$.

## Faster and faster

The further things fall, the more they accelerate and the faster they travel. Drop three equally sized plasticine balls from heights of 0.5m, 1m and 1.5m. When they land they dent. Which one has the biggest dent? Why do you think this is? (See page 47 to find out.)

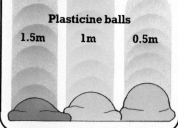

**Plasticine balls**

1.5m          1m          0.5m

# The Earth and the Moon

The Moon (like all satellites) circles around the Earth, keeping the same distance away and travelling at the same speed. It doesn't need a force to push it round as in space there is no friction at all, so once it is going at a certain speed it will continue for ever. It is kept the same distance from Earth all the time because of the Earth's strong gravitational pull.

**Moon**

**This distance hardly changes**

**Earth**

## Centrifugal force

"Centrifugal force" comes from the Latin words meaning "centre" and "flee". As a swing roundabout turns, the ropes pull inwards, keeping the swings from flying off in a straight line. The swings pull outwards on the ropes with a centrifugal ("centre-fleeing") force.

Try whirling a bucket of water round your head fast (outdoors, just in case it spills). The water doesn't fall out as it is all pushed back by the centrifugal force.

**Perhaps you can work out what forces are pushing on the parachute.**

## Making cream

People in industry use centrifugal force to separate different liquids such as milk and cream. Cream is less dense than

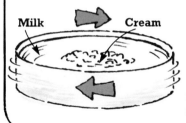

**Milk**          **Cream**

milk, so it needs less centrifugal force to carry on going round in a circle. There is less centrifugal force in the centre, so the cream stays here and the milk is pushed out to the sides.

## Terminal speed

Because of the forces of air resistance, something falling a long way, such as a parachutist, will accelerate to its terminal speed and will not be able to accelerate any more.

29

# Machines, work and power

You use machines all the time to help you do things. Some are things you may not think of as machines, such as nutcrackers and tin-openers. Machines help you to do "work". Work has a special meaning in science – it is only done when something is moved. So although you may think you have "worked hard" for a test, you have in fact done very little work in the scientific sense. The amount of work done (in joules) is the force moved (in newtons) multiplied by the distance moved (metres).

## Levers

Levers are a kind of simple machine. To a physicist, the ends of a see-saw are levers, and each person is trying to lift the other. A see-saw works best if the people are about the same weight and they sit at the ends. If one person is much heavier than the other, the heavier person needs to move nearer to the middle of the see-saw until the two people balance each other.

Ruler

Distance     Distance

Jar

Weight          Weight

Balance two things, one heavier than the other, on a ruler that is balanced on the side of a jar. The heavier thing will have to be much nearer the middle, or pivot, of the see-saw. Calculate the work being done on each side of the see-saw. Does one side equal the other?

In order to have perfect balance, the work being done on each side of the see-saw must be equal. This means the distance from each person to the middle of the see-saw multiplied by that person's weight has to be the same.

All levers have three parts: the fulcrum, which is the pivot where movement takes place; the load arm, which is the length of lever between the load and the fulcrum; and the force arm, which is the length of lever between the applied force and the fulcrum.

A wheelbarrow is a simple lever system. The wheel is the fulcrum about which the load moves. The load placed in the wheelbarrow acts downwards, while the gardener lifts upwards on the handles. The load arm is measured from the wheel to the load.

If the force (effort) arm is four times as long as the load arm, the upward lift needed on the handles is equal to a quarter of the downward load or weight in the barrow. So the gardener can carry a much greater load in a wheelbarrow than he could carry in his arms.

Effort

Fulcrum

Force arm

Load arm     Load

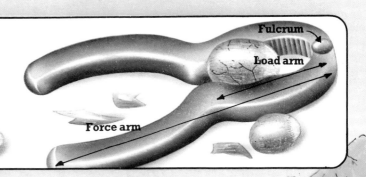

A nutcracker is also a lever. The big difference in the lengths of load arm and force arm means the pressure you exert on the handles is multiplied greatly and you are able to crack the hard nut.

**Fulcrum**

**Load arm**

**Force arm**

## Inclined planes

It is much easier to walk up a gentle hill than a very steep hill, which is why there are usually zig zag roads up mountains. A slope, or "inclined plane" is a kind of machine. Try and think of other ways of using an inclined plane to make your work easier.

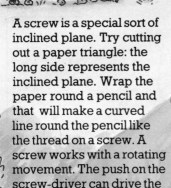

A screw is a special sort of inclined plane. Try cutting out a paper triangle: the long side represents the inclined plane. Wrap the paper round a pencil and that will make a curved line round the pencil like the thread on a screw. A screw works with a rotating movement. The push on the screw-driver can drive the screw deep into wood.

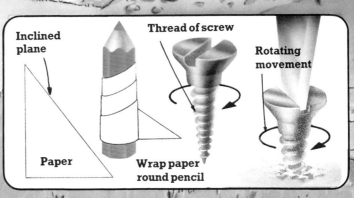

**Inclined plane**

**Thread of screw**

**Rotating movement**

**Paper**

**Wrap paper round pencil**

## How much work do you do?

You can measure the amount of work you do going upstairs by measuring the height of the stairs and multiplying it by your weight in newtons*.

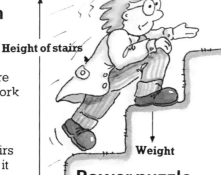

**Height of stairs**

**Weight**

If you run up the stairs very fast, you will have done the same amount of work as before but in less time. Power is the rate of doing work, and is calculated by dividing the work you do (in joules) by the time you take to do it (in seconds). Power is measured in joules per second, or watts.

## Power puzzle

If you weigh 450 newtons and climb up stairs 10 metres high in 2 seconds, how much work and power have you used?

31

*See page 22 to find out about your weight in newtons.

# Electricity and magnetism

Without electricity and magnetism, there would be no television, hi-fi systems, computers, video games, electric light and many of the other things around you. The next eight pages will tell you more about electricity and magnetism and how they work together.

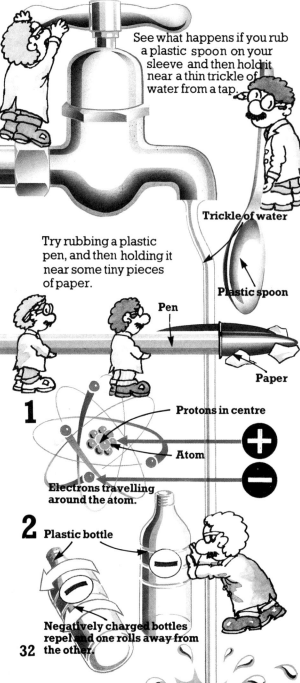

See what happens if you rub a plastic spoon on your sleeve and then hold it near a thin trickle of water from a tap.

**Trickle of water**

Try rubbing a plastic pen, and then holding it near some tiny pieces of paper.

**Plastic spoon**

**Pen**

**Paper**

**1**

**Protons in centre**

**Atom**

**Electrons travelling around the atom.**

**2** **Plastic bottle**

**Negatively charged bottles repel and one rolls away from the other.**

## Static electricity

When you undress, you can sometimes hear a crackling noise as something nylon rubs against another material. If it is dark, you can sometimes see tiny flashes of electricity. This happens because of static electricity.

The Ancient Greeks knew that static electricity existed, but it was not until the eighteenth century that Benjamin Franklin realized that there are two unlike charges of static electricity, which he called positive and negative. He was the first to discover that storm clouds are charged with static electricity, and he invented the lightning conductor in 1752.

Because of these electric charges, almost magical things can happen.

If you sit on a chair, rub your rubber-soled shoes on the carpet and then touch something metal, you may feel a tiny electric shock. This is because electric charges are flowing through your body.

## What is happening?

1. Everything is made up of atoms which themselves contain lots of charged particles. The positive charges are called protons and the negative charges electrons. In an uncharged (neutral) atom, the number of protons (+) is equal to the number of electrons (−). Electrons are much lighter than protons, and are on the edge of atoms, so they can move about. The protons are fixed in the centre or nucleus of the atom.

2. When two things such as wool and plastic are rubbed together, electrons sometimes move from one to the other. Rub two empty plastic bottles against wool. This makes them both negatively charged, with too many electrons. Put one on its side on a table, bring the second close to it, and the first bottle will roll away. Materials either negatively or positively charged can attract (pull) things that have an opposite charge. Materials having the same sort of charges repel (push) each other.

## Charged things with uncharged things

What happens if you put something you have charged, like the pen below, next to something uncharged, like paper? If the pen has a negative charge it will repel the electrons on the paper nearest to it. This will leave the paper with a positive charge at one end and so it will be attracted to the pen and stick to it.

Eventually some of the extra electrons on the pen will travel through you to the ground to be "earthed". The paper will not be attracted to the pen any more and will fall off.

**Negatively charged pen.**

**Paper eventually falls away from pen.**

**The protons on this side of the paper are attracted to the pen.**

**Negatively charged plastic bottle**

**Duck follows bottle**

## An electric question

Give an empty plastic bottle a negative charge by rubbing it with something woollen. Bring it close to a toy duck in the bath and the duck will follow behind the bottle. Why do you think this is? Find out on page 47. What would happen if you rubbed the duck with wool too?

*See page 34 for more about electric current and page 30 for more about work.

## Lightning

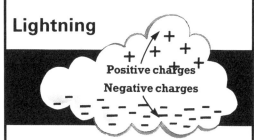

**Positive charges**

**Negative charges**

In thundery weather, clouds become charged by particles in them rubbing against each other. Positive and negative charges build up in different parts of the clouds until eventually a spark of negative charge leaps across from one side of the cloud to the other, making "sheet" lightning.

A very big charge on the cloud can "induce" an opposite charge on the Earth below. An electric current* then flows towards the Earth, making a flash of fork lightning. It lasts only a very short time, but a great amount of work* is done (about enough to run a 100W electric light bulb for a month). The air through which the current passes becomes very hot, but it returns to normal very quickly.

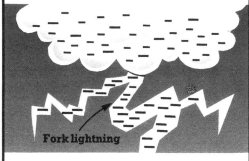

**Fork lightning**

If the electric current hits anything on its way to Earth, it burns it. High buildings have lightning conductors on them – strips of highly conductive metal – which take the current safely down to Earth.

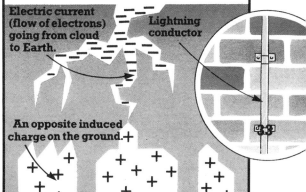

**Electric current (flow of electrons) going from cloud to Earth.**

**Lightning conductor**

**An opposite induced charge on the ground.**

# Current electricity

Static electricity means charges that stay still; they don't travel along wires or through the air. Current electricity is charges that are continuously on the move and it is this kind of electricity which makes things like light bulbs work. Power stations circulate electric current along the mains wires to the places that need current electricity.*

## Conductors and insulators

Like heat, electricity travels better through some materials than others. Good conductors of electricity have many more "free" electrons than insulators. Under normal conditions these electrons drift to and fro from atom to atom in a random way. Metals have lots of free electrons, which is why they are good conductors.

**Copper (good conductor) inside.**

**Insulator**

If you look at a piece of electrical flex you will find one, two or more copper wires (good conductors) wrapped in rubber (an insulator) in order to insulate the wires and make them safe.

WARNING!

The electricity in your home is very dangerous. Never touch the metal prongs in plugs, because electric current could flow through the prongs and through you. It could give your heart such a shock that it could stop beating.

Whenever there are more electrons at one end than at the other end of a conductor, free electrons in the conductor are forced to move one way, as an electric current, towards the end with fewer electrons. The difference in electrons between one end and the other is called the potential difference and is measured in volts. A battery can set up a potential difference. Current is a measure of the number of electrons drifting along the wire, and is measured in amperes (or amps).

## How a battery works

Inside a battery is a special chemical paste called the electrolyte that can conduct electricity. It is made of billions of positive and negative particles. The case of the battery is made of zinc and a carbon rod lies in the electrolyte. The zinc and carbon are both electrodes. A chemical reaction in the electrolyte sends positive particles to one electrode (the less reactive one) and negative particles to the other.

**Carbon rod**

**Zinc case**

**Electrolyte**

**Connection to metal part of torch.**

When the electrodes are connected by touching metal parts of a torch, electric current flows. When the electrolyte is used up, the current cannot flow any more and the battery is "dead".

## Make your own battery

**Drawing pin (brass)**     **Paper clip (steel)**

**Copper wire**

Stick two pieces of metal that are different into a lemon, making sure they are not touching each other. Wrap some copper wire around the ends of the metals, and connect the other ends of the wire to a 1.5 volt torch bulb which is in a lampholder. The lamp may light up. This is because the metals are acting as electrodes, and the lemon as the electrolyte.

34

*On page 42 there is a computer program which you can run to work out how much electricity you use at home, and how much your electricity bill will be.

# Electrical resistance

**Long wire**

**Short wire**

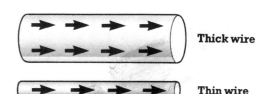

**Thick wire**

**Thin wire**

Good conductors of electricity allow electrons to flow easily. Sometimes, though, they bump into atoms in the wire and this slows them down. This braking effect is called the wire's resistance. The longer the piece of wire, the more resistance it has.

A thick wire has a lower resistance than a thin wire. There is a larger area of wire for the electrons to pass along. It is a bit like a motorway that can carry more traffic than a single-lane country road.

# Electric light

The wire in an electric light bulb is made of very thin, coiled tungsten metal. (Tungsten is used because it won't melt unless it gets very hot.) The electrons hit atoms in the wire, making them vibrate more and more and get hotter and hotter, until the wire glows with the "white heat" which we see as light.

**Electrons passing along the very fine wire keep bumping into atoms. The atoms vibrate, and give off heat and light.**

**Glass bulb**

**Wires support the filament**

**Coiled filament**

**A number in watts (W) telling you how much power the bulb uses and how brightly it glows. The bigger the number the brighter the glow, and the more electricity it uses.**

## Two sorts of electric current

The electric current a battery makes is called direct current (d.c.). It only flows in one direction. But the electric current that comes from power stations travels as "alternating current" (a.c.) which changes direction a hundred times a second. Alternating current can be transformed (using a "transformer") into higher voltages before it is sent over long distances. At high voltages less energy is lost as heat on the way.

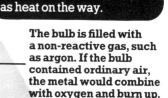

**The bulb is filled with a non-reactive gas, such as argon. If the bulb contained ordinary air, the metal would combine with oxygen and burn up.**

**Because the wire is tightly coiled, more wire can be put in the bulb, and more light is produced.**

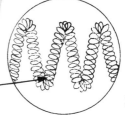

**Close up of coiled tungsten wire (called the filament).**

# Magnetism

Magnets are very useful to us. They are an essential part of loudspeakers, microphones, electric motors, door bells and many other things.

Magnetism was first discovered 2,500 years ago in a stone called lodestone, which people used to make the first compasses. Only the metals iron, nickel and cobalt can be magnetized on their own, but powerful magnets can be made by mixing these with other metals. Steel is iron with a little carbon in it, so it makes strong magnets too. See if you can find a magnet and find out what sorts of things it can pick up.

## Destroying magnetism

When something is magnetized, many of its molecules are pointing the same way. To destroy magnetism, you need to mix up all the "molecular magnets" again. You can do this by hitting a magnet with a hammer, or heating it until it is red-hot and letting it cool down (don't do this yourself).

## What is a magnet?

Imagine lots of matches representing groups of molecules* in a magnetic substance. Each matchstick is like a little magnet with a north pole at its head end and a south pole at the other end.

A bar of unmagnetized iron can be thought of as a jumble of matchstick magnets, so mixed up that all their magnetic forces cancel out.

When the iron bar is magnetized, many of the molecular magnets line up, with their north poles pointing the same way.

## Fields of force

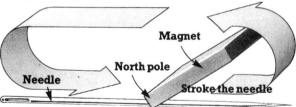

You can't see what makes magnets work, but there are magnetic forces around them and you can see the pattern they make by using iron filings. Put about one teaspoonful of filings into a box and shake it around so they cover the bottom. Hold the box just above a magnet, tap the box and you will see the filings jump up. They fall down into a pattern made up of curved lines. This pattern is called a field of force. These lines of force show what

**Iron filings**

happens in the space round a magnet. Try doing this with two magnets, their like poles together.

## Make a magnet

Playing with two bar magnets, you will find that a north pole will attract (pull) a south pole. Two "like poles" – south/south or north/north – repel (push) each other. You can magnetize a steel needle by stroking it in the same direction eight or nine times with the north pole of a bar magnet. As you do this, the north pole of the magnet pulls the south poles of the tiny molecular

magnets in the needle and makes them start to line up. See if the needle can pick things up now. If not, stroke it some more.

**Magnet**

**North pole**

**Needle**

**Stroke the needle**

*See page 14 for more about molecules.

# Electricity and magnetism

It was first noticed 150 years ago that when some small compasses are placed near a wire carrying an electric current, the needles lie in the direction of rings around the wire. As soon as the current is turned off the needles move back to their original north-south positions. The electric current makes a force field around the wire in the same way that a magnet would do.

**Wire carrying electric current.**

**Compasses**

## Electromagnets

A coil of wire called a solenoid can make a much stronger magnetic field than a single piece of wire. If an iron rod is placed inside the coil it behaves as if it is a very strong magnet while the current is switched on. When the current is switched off the iron stops being a magnet. This sort of magnet is called an electromagnet. Very big electromagnets are used to load and transport scrap iron, steel bars and machine parts. To pick metal up the current is turned on and to drop it again the current is switched off. Electromagnets are temporary magnets.

**Electromagnet**

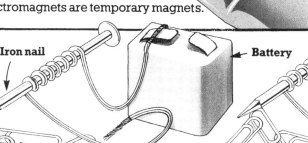

**Iron nail**

**Battery**

**Wire**

## Make an electromagnet

You can make your own electromagnet with some wire, a battery and an iron nail. Wind the wire around the nail, keeping the coils very close together. The more coils there are, the stronger the magnet will be. Twist the ends of the wire around the two terminals of the battery to make the electricity from the battery flow around the wire.

The nail becomes a magnet. You can test with some paper clips to see how strong it is. By undoing one of the terminals of the battery the nail stops being a magnet again.

## Another way of making magnets

**Only temporary magnets are made by "induction."**

A magnet can sometimes make something else into a magnet without even touching it. Its lines of force stretch out across space and make the "magnet-molecules" in the object line up. This is called magnetic induction.

# Electric motors

Imagine a wire carrying an electric current, placed between two magnets. The magnetic fields from the magnet interact with the electrical magnetic field from the wire. The force that results moves the wire to a new position. Electric motors use this idea.

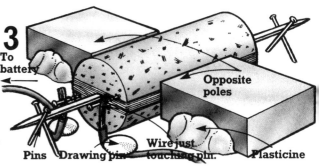

**3**
To battery

Opposite poles

Pins    Drawing pins    Wire just touching pin.    Plasticine

## Make an electric motor

It may help you to understand electric motors better if you build one yourself. You will need:
2 permanent magnets
1 large cork
6 pins
1 knitting needle
some thin, insulated copper wire
plasticine
soft board (fibreboard)
4½ volt battery
2 pieces of thicker, insulated copper wire
a sharp knife
2 drawing pins

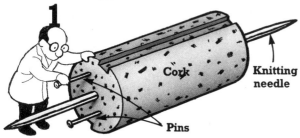

**1**

Cork    Knitting needle

Pins

Cut a narrow channel on either side of the cork. Push the knitting needle through the centre of the cork and push two pins into one end of the cork.

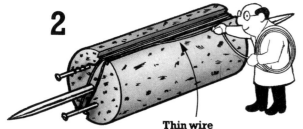

**2**

Thin wire

Strip about 2cm of the insulation off one end of the thin wire. Wrap it round one of the pins. Wind the wire round the cork about 30 times. Strip the insulation off the other end and wind it round the other pin.

Push two pairs of pins into the board so the knitting needle can rest in them like a cradle. Strip the insulation from the ends of the thicker copper wires. Use drawing pins to hold them so they just touch the pins in the cork.

Use plasticine to support the magnets on each side of the coil, with opposite poles facing. Connect the wires to a 4½ volt battery and give the cork a flick to start it going round.

## What is happening?

There are two separate fields of force working together in the motor. These diagrams show what happens to the field pattern. Imagine the wire carrying the current is sticking straight out of the page towards you.

**The two magnets, with their opposite poles together, set up fields of force that cross in the space between them, like this:**

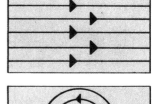

**Each wire makes its own field of force, like this:**

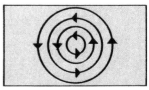

**The combined force looks like this. It has a "catapult" effect on the wire, pushing it to one side. In the motor this has the effect of pushing one side of the coil up and the other side down, which means the coil will rotate.**

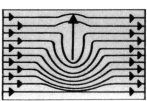

Electric motors are used to do many useful jobs of work; in vacuum cleaners, drills, trains, lifts and washing machines for instance. The motor is using electrical energy to do "work" (i.e. drive a machine).

# How loudspeakers work

Loudspeakers use a combination of magnetic and electric fields to bring speech and music into your home, and to carry your voice over the telephone. They convert electrical energy into sound energy.

A loudspeaker contains a movable coil of wire, attached to a large cone. The coil fits loosely over the centre of a cylindrical permanent magnet so that the coil is in a strong magnetic field.

Varying electric currents pass through the coil of wire. Because of the catapult effect (as in the electric motor), the coil moves. The cone is connected to the coil so it moves too, sending out vibrations (sound waves) into the air. The vibrations vary with the current.

It is the combination of the magnetic and electric fields that produces the movement of the coil and the cone, to send out the sound waves.

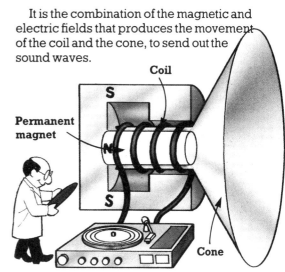

Coil

Permanent magnet

Cone

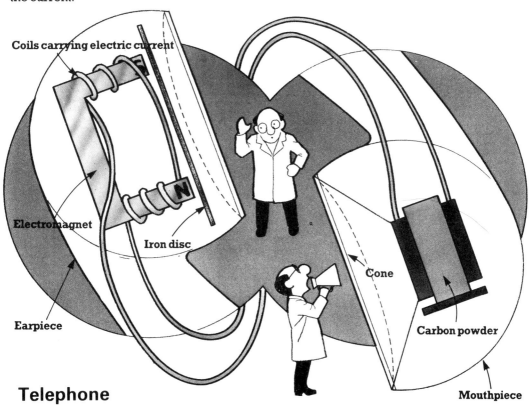

Coils carrying electric current

Electromagnet

Iron disc

Cone

Earpiece

Carbon powder

Mouthpiece

# Telephone

Here the varying electric currents pass round the coils of an electromagnet, which attracts an iron disc. As the currents vary, the movement of the disc varies and makes a sound wave in the air.

The varying electric currents are produced by a carbon microphone in the mouthpiece of a telephone. The sound waves force a cone in and out. This squeezes some carbon powder, through which the electric current is flowing. When the carbon is squeezed, its resistance is less and so the current passing through it changes as the sound wave changes.

**39**

# Electromagnetic spectrum

You have already found that light energy travels in electromagnetic waves. But there is a wide range of other electromagnetic waves too. Together they make up the electromagnetic spectrum. All these waves travel at the same speed – the speed of light, which is 300 million metres per second. The difference between them is in their varying wavelengths and in the way they affect things.

## Gamma rays

Gamma rays have the tiniest wavelength of all the electromagnetic waves. They are given off by some substances, for example uranium, which are radioactive. Radioactive substances are constantly giving out energy from the nuclei of their atoms, either in the form of particles, or as gamma rays. These rays are very penetrating, they can even travel through cement and lead. They can be very dangerous because they damage the cells of our bodies.

## X-rays

These were discovered accidentally in 1895 by a German physicist called Röntgen. He called them "X-the-unknown" because he didn't fully understand them. To produce X-rays, a beam of electrons is fired at a heavy target, usually made of tungsten.

Your body tissue is mostly made up of hydrogen, oxygen, carbon and nitrogen, but your bones contain calcium, which is denser and absorbs rays better. When X-rays are shone through your body most of them go right through and fall onto a photographic plate on the other side, but where there are bones the rays are stopped and this makes a shadow on the plate. From this doctors can tell if a bone is broken or out of place. They can also see accidentally swallowed objects.

## Ultraviolet waves

These are beyond the violet end of the visible light spectrum; we can't see them, but most insects can. They usually come from the Sun and most of them are absorbed by the layer of ozone that surrounds the Earth. Ultraviolet waves make you sun-tanned, but if you stay in the Sun too long they are dangerous, because you get sunburnt. When you lie on a "sunbed" you are getting tanned by artificially produced ultraviolet light.

## Visible light

Turn to page 6 to find out more about visible light.

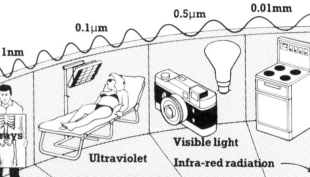

0.1µm  0.5µm  0.01mm

1nm

Short wavelength  X-rays

0.01nm

Special machines detecting gamma rays

Gamma rays

Visible light

Ultraviolet

Infra-red radiation

## Infra-red radiation

Infra-red radiation has longer wavelengths than red light. We cannot see it, but we feel it as heat. We call it heat radiation because it is given off by most hot things. Only the infra-red rays near the visible spectrum pass through glass, the longer ones are absorbed by it.

## Microwaves

Microwaves have wavelengths between 1mm and 0.3m, which is between infra-red radiation and radio waves. Radar, which is a way of locating a distant object, uses microwaves. The waves are fired at the object, and some are reflected back. From the time it takes for them to come back, it can be worked out how far away the object is and how far it is moving.

Microwave "ovens" are used to heat and cook food very quickly. The waves give the molecules in the food lots of energy, making the food so hot that even a potato can be baked in 4 minutes.

**40**

## TV and radio waves

Radio waves can be used to carry messages and television pictures around the world at the speed of light. Radio waves are grouped into bands and each band has a special set of uses. Cameras and microphones create electronic signals which are combined with radio waves and sent out to be picked up by aerials connected to people's TV sets.

Nowadays more and more TV programs are being transported through underground cables, rather than across space on electromagnetic waves. It is possible to send many more channels by cable without them interfering with each other.

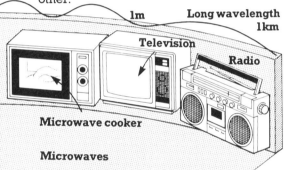

1m Long wavelength 1km
Television
Radio
Microwave cooker
Microwaves

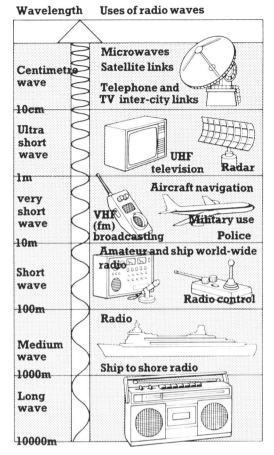

| Wavelength | Uses of radio waves |
|---|---|
| Centimetre wave | Microwaves Satellite links |
| | Telephone and TV inter-city links |
| 10cm | |
| Ultra short wave | UHF television  Radar |
| 1m | |
| very short wave | Aircraft navigation |
| | VHF (fm) broadcasting  Military use  Police |
| 10m | |
| Short wave | Amateur and ship world-wide radio |
| | Radio control |
| 100m | Radio |
| Medium wave | |
| 1000m | Ship to shore radio |
| Long wave | |
| 10000m | |

## Lasers

A laser is any device that emits beams of laser light, which is quite different from natural light in several ways. Laser light is very pure in colour because it contains a very narrow range of wavelengths. And it can be produced in a very parallel beam. Also, the light is polarized (that is, the waves, instead of vibrating in all directions at right angles to the direction of the beam, vibrate in just one of those directions). And some types of laser produce incredibly intense split-second pulses of light that can even vaporize metal.

The most common source of laser light is a crystal, such as a ruby, which can be stimulated by a flash of very bright light. A special mixture of gases can also give off laser light when an electric current passes through it.

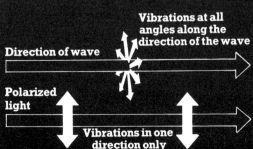

Vibrations at all angles along the direction of the wave
Direction of wave
Polarized light
Vibrations in one direction only

## Fibre optic cables

The latest development in cable systems is the use of fibre optic cables. These are made of bundles of very thin glass, down which is passed a pattern of laser light. Sound can be converted into patterns of laser light and transmitted in this way across very long distances.

# Home electricity computer program

This program works out how much electricity things like your television and cooker use. You can also calculate how much your three-monthly bill should add up to.

If you have, or can borrow, a BBC microcomputer, you can run the program as it is. Lines that need changing for other computers are marked with symbols and printed at the end of the program. Each symbol corresponds to a different computer. They are:

▲ VIC and PET
∎ ZX SPECTRUM, ZX81
● APPLE
■ TRS-80
○ ORIC

Before you can work out your bill you need to check on a recent electricity bill or ring up, to find out the unit price (UP) you pay for electricity.

Different computers vary too much to be able to give general instructions for graphics, but there is an example of a graphics subroutine for a light bulb, which will work on a Spectrum (Timex 2000). This should be added at the end of the program, and another line put into the program to call it up: 1675 GOSUB 3000.

You could perhaps try writing your own graphics routines for the other appliances.

```
 10 REM INITIALISE
 20 LET N=10: REM NO. OF APPLIANCES
 30 DIM U(N): REM UNITS USED
∎40 DIM A$(N): REM NAMES
 50 LET TU=0: REM POWER USED
 60 LET UP=2.5: REM UNIT PRICE
 70 LET A$(1)="COOKER"
 80 LET A$(2)="IMMERSION HEATER"
 90 LET A$(3)="FAN HEATER"
100 LET A$(4)="RADIANT HEATER"
110 LET A$(5)="LIGHT BULB"
120 LET A$(6)="WASHING MACHINE"
130 LET A$(7)="TELEVISION"
140 LET A$(8)="RADIO"
150 LET A$(9)="CONVECTOR HEATER"
160 LET A$(10)="HI-FI STEREO"
170 REM * PRINT INTRO PAGE *
180 CLS
190 PRINT
200 PRINT
210 PRINT "ELECTRICITY BILL"
```

```
220 PRINT "  CALCULATION"
230 PRINT "  ==========="
240 PRINT
250 PRINT "POWER"
260 PRINT "STATION >>>>>>>>>"
270 PRINT "            TRANS-"
280 PRINT "            FORMER"
290 FOR I=1 TO 4
300 PRINT "            V"
310 NEXT I
320 PRINT "            HOUSE"
330 PRINT
340 PRINT"PRESS SPACE TO START"
350 GOSUB 810
360 REM MAIN MENU PAGE
370 CLS
380 PRINT "CHOOSE THE APPLIANCE"
390 PRINT "THAT YOU WANT TO ENTER"
400 PRINT "NEXT, OR TYPE 0 TO"
410 PRINT "CALCULATE YOUR BILL"
420 PRINT
```

```
430 PRINT "                    UNITS"
440 FOR I=1 TO N
450 IF U(I)>0 THEN PRINT ;I;" ";A$(I);
    TAB (19);U(I)
460 IF U(I)=0 THEN PRINT ;I;" ";A$(I)
470 NEXT I
480 PRINT
490 PRINT "TYPE A NUMBER AND THEN"
500 PRINT "PRESS ENTER";
510 INPUT C
520 IF C<0 OR C>N THEN GOTO 360
530 IF C=0 THEN GOTO 580
540 CLS
550 PRINT
560 ON C GOSUB 1060,1280,1330,1530,1650,
    1700,1900,2060,2110,2160
570 GOTO 360
580 REM FINAL PAGE
590 CLS
600 FOR W=1 TO N
610 LET TU=TU+U(W)
620 NEXT W
630 PRINT
640 PRINT "ELECTRICITY BILL"
650 PRINT "   ESTIMATE"
660 PRINT "   ========"
670 PRINT "(FOR 3 MONTHS)"
680 PRINT
690 PRINT "UNITS USED :"
700 PRINT ;TU;" KILOWATT-HRS"
710 PRINT
720 PRINT "UNIT PRICE :";UP;" PENCE"
730 LET TC=(INT(UP*TU))/100
740 PRINT
750 PRINT
760 PRINT "TOTAL DUE : '";TC
770 PRINT
780 PRINT "PRESS SPACE TO RUN AGAIN"
790 GOSUB 810
800 RUN
810 LET I$=INKEY$(0)
820 IF I$<>" " THEN GOTO 810
830 RETURN
840 REM PAGE FOR INPUT
850 CLS
860 PRINT
870 PRINT N$
880 PRINT
890 PRINT ;P*1000;" WATTS"

900 FOR I=1 TO 7
910 PRINT
920 NEXT I
930 PRINT "HOW LONG IS THIS APPLIANCE"
940 PRINT "USED EACH WEEK, ON AVERAGE?"
950 PRINT "(IN HOURS)"
960 PRINT "TYPE THE NUMBER THEN"
970 PRINT "PRESS RETURN";
980 INPUT T
990 LET U(C)=U(C)+P*T*13
1000 RETURN
1010 REM MOVE DOWN 5 LINES
1020 FOR X=1 TO 5
1030 PRINT
1040 NEXT X
1050 RETURN
1060 REM * COOKER *
1070 PRINT A$(C)
1080 GOSUB 1010
1090 PRINT "PRESS  1) FOR RING"
1100 PRINT "       2) FOR OVEN"
1110 PRINT "       3) FOR GRILL"
1120 PRINT
1130 INPUT I
1140 IF I<1 OR I>3 THEN GOTO 1130
1150 ON I GOTO 1160,1200,1240
1160 LET N$="COOKER RING"
1170 LET P=1
1180 GOSUB 840
1190 RETURN
1200 LET N$="COOKER OVEN"
1210 LET P=3
1220 GOSUB 840
1230 RETURN
1240 LET N$="COOKER GRILL"
1250 LET P=1.5
1260 GOSUB 840
1270 RETURN
1280 REM * IMMERSION HEATER *
1290 LET N$=A$(C)
1300 LET P=3.5
1310 GOSUB 840
1320 RETURN
1330 REM * FAN HEATER *
1340 LET N$="FAN HEATER"
1350 PRINT N$
1360 GOSUB 1010
1370 PRINT "IS IT  1) FULL ON"
1380 PRINT "       2) HALF ON"
```

**43**

```
1390 PRINT "      3) COLD AIR"
1400 INPUT I
1410 IF I<1 OR I>3 THEN GOTO 1400
1420 ON I GOTO 1430,1460,1490
1430 LET N$=N$+" (FULL ON)"
1440 LET P=3
1450 GOTO 1510
1460 LET N$=N$+" (HALF ON)"
1470 LET P=1.5
1480 GOTO 1510
1490 LET N$=N$+" (COLD AIR)"
1500 LET P=0.3
1510 GOSUB 840
1520 RETURN
1530 REM * RADIANT HEATER *
1540 LET N$="RADIANT HEATER"
1550 PRINT N$
1560 GOSUB 1010
1570 PRINT "ARE YOU USING "
1580 PRINT "1,2 OR 3 BARS"
1590 INPUT I
1600 IF I<1 OR I>3 THEN GOTO 1590
1610 LET N$=N$+" ("+STR$(I)+" BARS)"
1620 LET P=I
1630 GOSUB 840
1640 RETURN
1650 REM * LIGHT BULB *
1660 LET N$=A$(C)
1670 LET P=0.1
1680 GOSUB 840
1690 RETURN
1700 REM * WASHING MACHINE *
1710 LET N$="WASHING MACHINE"
1720 PRINT N$
1730 GOSUB 1010
1740 PRINT "IS IT  1) WASHING"
1750 PRINT "       2) SPINNING"
1760 PRINT "       3) HEATING"
1770 INPUT I
1780 IF I<1 OR I>3 THEN GOTO 1770
1790 ON I GOTO 1800,1830,1860
1800 LET N$=N$+" (WASHING)"
1810 LET P=0.8
1820 GOTO 1880
1830 LET N$=N$+" (SPINNING)"
1840 LET P=0.8
1850 GOTO 1880
1860 LET N$=N$+" (HEATING)"
1870 LET P=3
1880 GOSUB 840
1890 RETURN
1900 REM * TELEVISION *
1910 LET N$="TELEVISION"
1920 PRINT N$
1930 GOSUB 1010
1940 PRINT "IS IT 1) COLOUR"
1950 PRINT "   OR 2) BLACK AND WHITE"
1960 INPUT I
1970 IF I<1 OR I>2 THEN GOTO 1960
1980 IF I=2 THEN GOTO 2020
1990 LET N$=N$+" (COLOUR)"
2000 LET P=0.4
2010 GOTO 2040
2020 LET N$=N$+" (BLACK AND WHITE)"
2030 LET P=0.3
2040 GOSUB 840
2050 RETURN
2060 REM * RADIO *
2070 LET N$=A$(C)
2080 LET P=0.05
2090 GOSUB 840
2100 RETURN
2110 REM * CONVECTOR HEATER *
2120 LET N$=A$(C)
2130 LET P=3
2140 GOSUB 840
2150 RETURN
2160 REM * HI-FI STEREO *
2170 LET N$=A$(C)
2180 LET P=0.15
2190 GOSUB 840
2200 RETURN
```

## Light bulb graphics

Below is a graphics subroutine for a
light bulb. It will only work on a
Spectrum (Timex 2000) and should be
added here. In order to call it up
another line must be put into the
program: 1675 GOSUB 3000.

```
3000 REM GRAPHICS FOR LIGHT BULB
3010 CLS : PLOT 175,40: DRAW 0,32:
     DRAW -8,32,.7: DRAW 48,0,-4.9:
     DRAW -8,-32,.7: DRAW 0,-32
3020 PLOT 184,40: DRAW -8,88,.2
3030 PLOT 199,40: DRAW 8,88,-.2
3040 PRINT AT 5,22; INK 6; BRIGHT 1;"****"
3050 RETURN
```

# Using different computers

Below is a list of changes that will enable you to run this program on other computers too. The symbols on the left-hand side of the column correspond to different computers. These instructions need to be inserted into the program in the relevant places.

```
■    40 DIM A$(10,16)
■   560 GOSUB 1060*(C=1)+1280*(C=2)+1330*(C=3
  )+1530*(C=4)+1650*(C=5)+1700*(C=6)+1900*(C=
  7)+2060*(C=8)+2110*(C=9)+2160*(C=10)
○   810 LET I$=KEY$
▲   810 GET I$
●   810 LET I$=""
●   812 IF PEEK(-16384)>127 THEN GET I$
■■  810 LET I$=INKEY$
■  1150 GOTO 1160*(I=1)+1200*(I=2)+1240*(I=3)
■  1420 GOTO 1430*(I=1)+1460*(I=2)+1490*(I=3)
■  1790 GOTO 1800*(I=1)+1830*(I=2)+1860*(I=3)
```

# Physics words

This is a selection of some of the most important physics words and laws. Some you will have met in this book already. You will find that they are useful to all sorts of people, not just students: computer engineers, mechanics, electricians, space scientists, radiographers, sound engineers and many other people need to know a bit of physics for their jobs.

**Acceleration.** The increase of velocity every second measured in metres per second per second, ($m/s^2$).

**Alternating current (a.c.).** An electric current that flows first in one direction, then in the other.

**Ampere (amp).** The quantity of electric current flowing every second.

**Amplitude.** The height of a wave.

**Archimedes Principle.** A body floating in a fluid displaces a weight of fluid equal to its own weight.

**Atom.** The smallest particle of an element that can take part in a chemical reaction.

**Centre of gravity.** The point at which the weight of a body appears to act.

**Conductor.** A substance or body that offers a relatively small resistance to the passage of an electric current, or to heat.

**Conservation of energy (law of).** In any closed system energy cannot be created or destroyed, although its form may be changed.

**Convection.** The transfer of heat in a fluid (or gas) by the movement of the fluid itself.

**Coulomb.** The unit of electric charge. One coulomb is the charge transported in one second by an electric current of one ampere.

**Critical angle.** The greatest angle of incidence at which light can escape from a denser medium into a less dense one (angle of refraction = $90°$).

**Current.** The rate of flow of electricity, measured in amperes.

**Decibel (dB).** The unit of the intensity ot sound.

**Density.** The mass per unit volume of a substance, often measured in kilograms per cubic metre ($kg/m^3$).

**Direct current (d.c.).** An electric current that flows in one direction only.

**Electron.** A negatively charged particle, present in all atoms. Free electrons are responsible for electrical conduction in most substances.

**45**

**Energy.** A measure of the capacity to do work, measured in joules (J).

**Force.** Any action that alters a body's state of rest or of uniform motion in a straight line. Measured in newtons (N).

**Frequency.** The number of waves or cycles in one second.

**Friction.** A force that occurs whenever two things rub together.

**Gravity.** The pulling force of the Earth.

**Incidence (angle of).** The angle between the ray striking a surface and the normal to the surface at the point of incidence.

**Inertia.** The property of a body whereby it persists in a state of rest or uniform motion in a straight line.

**Insulator.** A substance that provides high resistance to the passage of an electric current, or to heat.

**Joule (J).** The unit of energy. One joule is the work done when a force of 1 newton moves something through 1 metre distance.

**Kinetic energy (K.E.).** The energy of movement, measured in joules.

**Mass.** The amount of matter in a body measured in kilograms.

**Momentum.** The mass of a body multiplied by its velocity.

**Motor.** A machine that converts electrical energy into mechanical energy.

**Newton (N).** The unit of force. One newton provides a mass of 1 kg with an acceleration of $1 \, m/s^2$.

**Newton's laws of motion**
1. Every body remains in a state of rest or uniform motion in a straight line unless acted upon by forces from the outside.
2. The amount of acceleration of a body is proportional to the acting force and inversely proportional to the mass of the body.
3. Every action has an equal and opposite reaction.

**Ohm ($\Omega$).** The unit of resistance.

**Pascal (Pa).** The unit of pressure. One pascal is the pressure that results from a force of one newton acting on an area of one square metre. One pascal is equal to one newton per square metre ($N/m^2$).

**Pitch.** The pitch of sound depends on its frequency. High frequency = high pitch, low frequency = low pitch.

**Potential difference (p.d.).** The voltage in part of an electric circuit, measured in volts.

**Potential energy (P.E.).** Energy which is stored up, ready to be used, measured in joules (J).

**Power.** The rate energy is expended, or work is done. Power is measured in watts.

**Pressure.** The force per unit area. Measured in pascals, or newtons per square metre ($N/m^2$) or millimetres of mercury (mmHg).

**Proton.** A positively charged particle that is present in all nuclei.

**Radiation.** Any form of energy that moves as waves, rays or a stream of particles.

**Reflection (laws of)**
1. The incident ray, normal and the reflected ray all lie in the same plane.
2. The angle of incidence is equal to the angle of reflection.

**Refraction.** The change of direction that a ray undergoes when it enters another transparent substance.

**Resistance.** The more resistance a wire has, the less current it can carry. Resistance is measured in ohms.

**Transformer.** A device that alters the alternating voltage of an electric current.

**Velocity.** The speed of a body in a particular direction measured in metres per second (m/s).

**Volt.** One volt is the force needed to carry one ampere of current against one ohm of resistance.

**Watt.** The unit of power. One watt is the power resulting from the dissipation of one joule of energy in one second. In electricity watts = amps × volts.

**Wavelength.** Length from one peak in a series of waves to the next.

**Weight.** The force exerted on matter by the gravitational pull of the Earth, measured in newtons (N).

**Important physics equations**
Force (N) = mass (kg) × acceleration (m/s$^2$)
Volts = current (amps) × resistance (ohms)
Velocity of a wave (m/s) = frequency × wavelength (m)
Pressure (N/m$^2$) = force (N) ÷ area (m$^2$)
Power (watts) = volts × current (amps)
1m = 1,000,000 $\mu$m (micrometres)
= 1,000,000,000 nm (nanometres)

# Answers

## Page 5: Energy puzzle
1. Here the dog has potential chemical and gravitational energy.
2. When running downstairs, the dog is changing potential energy to kinetic (movement) energy.
3. At the bottom of the stairs, the food the dog eats is replacing some of the chemical potential energy that changed to kinetic energy when he came downstairs.

## Page 6: Light energy
The Sun, a torch and a candle are sources of light, the other things are only reflecting light that comes from another source. Even the Moon is only reflecting the Sun's light.

## Page 20
The flute produces music by blowing. The piano has little hammers inside that hit the strings.
The violin and harp both have strings that are plucked.

## Page 22
If your mass is 60kg you would weigh 100N on the Moon, and your mass would be the same on the Moon as on the Earth.

## Page 24
The water molecules on the surface of the water on the paintbrush pull together strongly because there are no molecules outside to pull on. So the bristles are pulled together too.

## Page 28
The plasticine ball that falls the greatest distance will have the biggest dent. It has had more time to accelerate and will hit the ground at a greater speed than the others.

## Page 31: Power puzzle
The work done by climbing stairs 10 metres high in 2 seconds, when you weigh 450 newtons = 450 × 10 = 4500 joules. The power used is 4500 ÷ 2 = 2250 watts.

## Page 33: An electric question
When the negatively charged bottle is brought near to the plastic duck, the negative charges in the duck will be repelled. The negative charges move to the far end of the duck, leaving positive charges near the bottle. These will be attracted by the bottle, and the duck will follow the bottle. If the duck is negatively charged too, it will move away from the bottle.

### Going further:

Books to read:

*Physics Alive*
by Peter Warren
(John Murray)

*Physics for You 1 & 2*
by Keith Johnson
(Hutchinson)

*The Young Scientist Book of Electricity*
by Phil Chapman
(Usborne)

*Physics for All*
by J. J. Wellington
(ST(P))

# Index

# INTRODUCTION TO
# CHEMISTRY

## Jane Chisholm and Mary Johnson
### Consultant editor: Alan Alder
### Designed by Iain Ashman

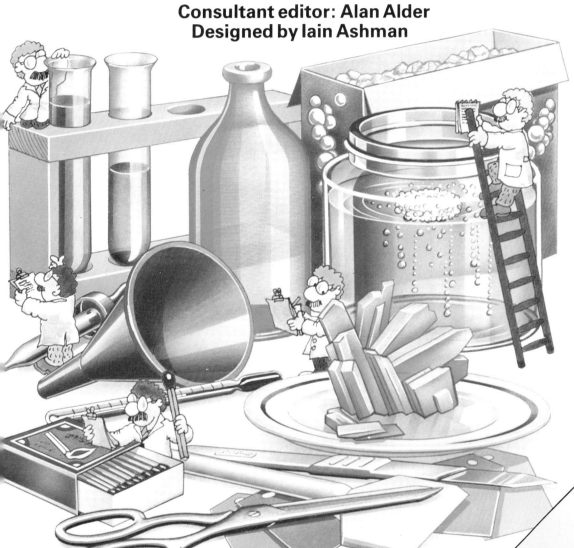

Illustrated by Jeremy Banks, Sue Stitt, Chris Lyon,
Jeremy Gower, Graham Smith, Graham Round,
Simon Roulstone and Penny Simon

Computer program by Chris Oxlade

WITH
COMPUTER
PROGRAM LISTING

# Chemistry contents

# About this section of the book

This section contains a general introduction to the basic ideas of chemistry. It begins by looking at atoms and molecules and some of the ideas that chemistry is based on. This will help you understand what is going on in chemical reactions and why.

There are lots of experiments for you to try out if you want to. Don't worry if you find an experiment doesn't work first time. This can often happen, even to very experienced chemists. There are lots of resons why an experiment might go wrong – just try again. On page 92, there are tips on safety, and on getting the best results from your experiments. There's advice too on where to get hold of chemicals and other equipment.

At the end of this section, you can find the answers to puzzles and questions. There are also definitions of difficult or unfamiliar "chemistry" words, as well as useful charts and summaries. Chemists write down chemical reactions in "formulae" and "equations". You can find out about writing equations at the end too.

If you have a home computer, or can borrow one from someone, there's a program to try out. It helps you identify unknown chemicls and is written to work on most common makes of home computer.

# What is chemistry?

Chemistry is the study of chemicals. Everything around you is made of chemicals – the land, sea, sky, houses, cars, food, clothes and even your body.

There are just over a hundred basic chemicals. These are called elements. You will have heard of some of them already, such as gold or oxygen. Elements are the building bricks of chemistry. Although they can exist on their own, they are usually combined with other elements.

By studying what things are made of, and how they react with other things, chemists can work out how to make new, useful substances. Here are some of the things that chemists have invented or developed.

**Medicines**

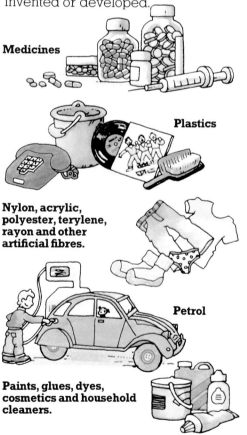

**Plastics**

**Nylon, acrylic, polyester, terylene, rayon and other artificial fibres.**

**Petrol**

**Paints, glues, dyes, cosmetics and household cleaners.**

**Fertilizers**

Chemicals in laboratories may not seem very interesting, but, put together with other chemicals, they can produce all kinds of reactions – bangs, whizzes, flashes – and new chemicals are formed.

There are chemical reactions going on all around you – when you do the washing up, or strike a match, or cook something.

Rust and buildings, blackened and worn away with age, are signs of chemical reactions too.

Your body is a bit like a large, rubbery test tube, with lots of chemical reactions going on inside. You add more chemicals – food and oxygen from the air – to keep all these reactions going.

**51**

# How chemistry began

Chemistry comes from the Arabic, *al quemia*, meaning alchemy. Alchemy was an early form of chemistry, which began about 2,000 years ago. Alchemists began by trying to turn ordinary metals into gold. There was often a lot of magic and superstition involved. Alchemy was not a real science, although some scientific methods were used. They made some important discoveries, such as how to make medicines and drugs from herbs.

Modern chemistry probably began in the 17th century, when Robert Boyle defined elements. Another important step came in 1808, with John Dalton's atomic theory. He said that elements could be divided into tiny particles, called atoms. Ideas such as these provide the framework for modern chemistry.

## How chemists work

A lot of science involves using ideas that have not yet been proved. In order to predict or guess what is going to happen in a reaction or how a chemical is going to behave, the chemist will make an intelligent guess, called a hypothesis. This hypothesis is then tested in many experiments. It cannot be conclusively proved true, but if it is never disproved, it becomes accepted and can be used in explaining discoveries and forming new hypotheses.

Chemistry involves studying tiny, but complicated particles. To describe them, chemists use simplified diagrams, like this one of an atom. No-one pretends that atoms actually look like this, but it shows the parts the chemist is interested in.

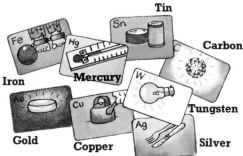

Iron
Tin
Mercury
Carbon
Gold
Copper
Silver
Tungsten

Chemists have developed their own language, which is understood all over the world. It involves writing in "formulae". Each element has a symbol, consisting of one or two letters. You can guess some of them, because they start with the first letter of the element's name (sometimes its Latin or Greek name).

Chemistry experiments can easily go wrong unless they are done very carefully. This is why chemists work in laboratories. There they can control the temperature, weigh things on very accurate scales, and carry out experiments in safe and controlled conditions.

# Looking at chemicals

Chemists try to sort everything into groups, in order to make their work easier. There are lots of different ways of classifying chemicals. You can divide them into solids, liquids and gases, or into metals and non-metals. If you want to classify something, you can start by looking at its physical characteristics – or "properties", as chemists call them. Here are the sorts of questions that a chemist would ask.

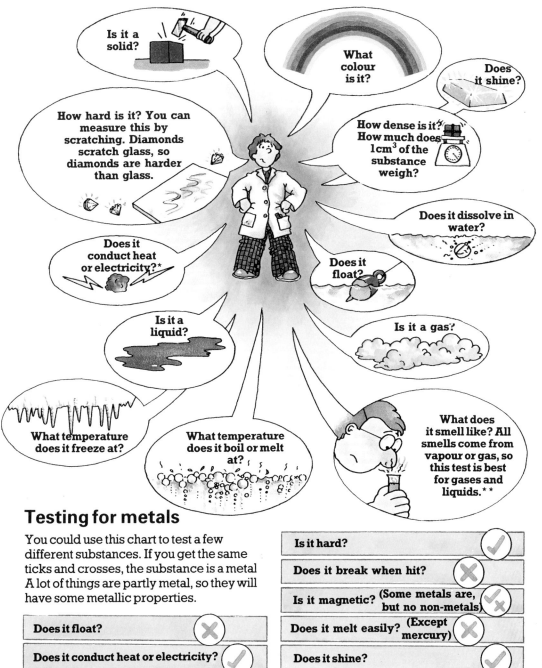

Is it a solid?

What colour is it?

Does it shine?

How hard is it? You can measure this by scratching. Diamonds scratch glass, so diamonds are harder than glass.

How dense is it? How much does 1cm$^3$ of the substance weigh?

Does it dissolve in water?

Does it conduct heat or electricity?*

Does it float?

Is it a liquid?

Is it a gas?

What temperature does it freeze at?

What temperature does it boil or melt at?

What does it smell like? All smells come from vapour or gas, so this test is best for gases and liquids.**

## Testing for metals

You could use this chart to test a few different substances. If you get the same ticks and crosses, the substance is a metal. A lot of things are partly metal, so they will have some metallic properties.

| Is it hard? | ✓ |
| Does it break when hit? | ✗ |
| Is it magnetic? (Some metals are, but no non-metals) | ✓✗ |
| Does it melt easily? (Except mercury) | ✗ |
| Does it shine? | ✓ |

| Does it float? | ✗ |
| Does it conduct heat or electricity? | ✓ |

53

*You can find out how to test this on page 66.
**Be careful! It's dangerous to get too close to a lot of chemicals.

# What things are made of

Scientists believe that absolutely everything is made of particles. Imagine a piece of an element, such as copper. If it were possible to go on cutting it into smaller and smaller pieces, you would eventually get a tiny particle called an atom. An atom is the smallest particle that can have the chemical properties of a particular element. The word comes from the Greek, *atomos*, meaning "indivisible". We can't see atoms properly, but knowing about them will help you understand chemical reactions better.

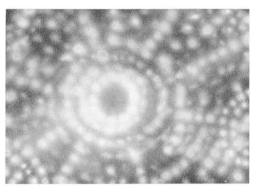

This is part of the tip of a needle, magnified about three million times. It is seen through a very powerful machine called a field-ion microscope. Each spot of light represents an atom.

## Inside an atom

Each atom is a bit like a miniature solar system, with a nucleus in the middle and particles called electrons orbiting around outside it. All the atoms of an element are different from the atoms of other elements, and have different numbers of electrons. Atoms have lots of other particles too, but many of these have only recently been discovered and scientists don't yet know as much about them.

**1** Electrons are particles with a negative electric charge. They travel round the nucleus in orbits.

**2** Each atom of an element has a certain number of electrons. This is called its atomic number.

**3** The electrons of an atom are arranged in different layers, or orbits. You can find out more about these on page 16.

**4** Chemists believe that electrons usually spin in pairs. One goes clockwise, the other, anti-clockwise.

**5** Chemists used to think that electrons moved in fixed orbits, like planets. They now believe that electrons can be anywhere within their orbit, at any time. Sometimes they may even be outside it. However, this would be very difficult to draw, so electron orbits are usually shown like this.

**6** Atoms of different elements have a different size and weight. Chemists call this their "mass". We cannot weigh atoms, but we can work out their mass in comparison with other atoms. This is called the relative atomic mass. It is based on an atom of carbon, which is said to have a mass of 12.

# Radioactivity

Since the beginning of this century, scientists have known that atoms could be split. The nucleus of an atom contains a great deal of energy. Some isotopes of certain atoms have unstable nuclei,* which may fall apart giving off energy and radiation. They are called radioactive isotopes.

**Nuclear power station**

**Archaeological site**

Atoms can be split artificially too. The energy can be trapped and used to provide light and heat. This is what nuclear power stations do. However this radiation, although invisible, is extremely dangerous. It is the basis of nuclear weapons.

Ordinary atoms go on forever, but radioactive ones have a fixed life-span. This can be seconds, or millions of years. Carbon 14** is slightly radioactive and disintegrates very slowly. It is used to work out the age of archaeological finds.

**10** Usually all the atoms of an element have the same mass number, but some do not. These are called the different isotopes of an element.

**9** The number of protons and neutrons added together is called the mass number of an atom

Most of an atom consists of empty space. Imagine the nucleus as the size of a pea in an international football pitch. Some of the electrons would be orbiting at the very edge of the stadium.

**8** The nucleus also contains a number of uncharged, neutral particles, called neutrons.

**11** Atoms are held together by the strong attraction between the protons and electrons. Particles with opposite charges attract one another, like opposite poles of a magnet.

**7** The nucleus contains particles called protons, which have a positive electric charge. Atoms have the same number of protons as electrons. This makes them electrically neutral. Protons are about 1,840 times heavier than electrons.

55

\*\**This means it has a mass number of 14, instead of 12, which most carbon atoms have.*
\**Plural of nucleus.*

# Looking at particles

Looking at how atoms behave can help you understand more about chemical reactions. Atoms rarely exist on their own. They usually group together in particles called molecules, or in giant structures called lattices.

A molecule is the smallest particle of a substance that can normally exist by itself. Hydrogen and oxygen atoms, for example, go around in pairs. So a molecule of hydrogen contains two atoms. Chemists write this as $H_2$, to show that there are two atoms.

Other molecules are made up of larger numbers of atoms. For example, phosphorus molecules contain four atoms. Sulphur molecules contain eight atoms in a ring.

Molecules of compounds contain different types of atoms bonded together in fixed proportions. Here are the molecules of a few different compounds. Their formulae show you how many atoms of each element there are in the molecule.

## Solids, liquids and gases

Chemists call solids, liquids and gases the three states of matter. Any substance can change from one state to another, depending on its temperature and pressure. The difference between these states lies in how much the particles in the substance are moving around and how tightly packed together they are.

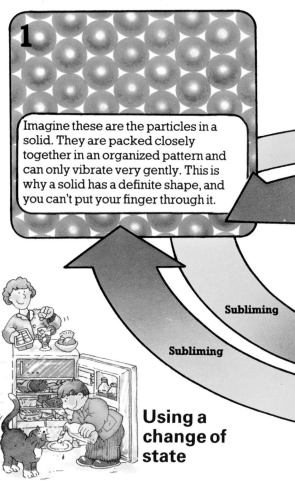

**1** Imagine these are the particles in a solid. They are packed closely together in an organized pattern and can only vibrate very gently. This is why a solid has a definite shape, and you can't put your finger through it.

Subliming

Subliming

## Using a change of state

Inside the back of a fridge is a liquid which boils and turns into a gas at a very low temperature. But in order to do this, it needs energy. It gets this energy by taking heat away from the inside of the fridge. As it does so, the fridge becomes much colder than the rest of the room. This keeps the food cool. At the back of the fridge is a "condenser", where the gas changes back into a liquid. As it does this, heat is given out from the back of the fridge.

**2**

When particles are close together, they attract one another. So a lot of energy is needed to push them apart. Heat is a form of energy. When you heat a solid, it gives the particles energy. They start vibrating a lot and move away from each other. This is why things melt when you heat them. Chemists call this a change of state.

## Changes of state

When something changes state, heat is always produced or lost. As water gets colder, it freezes into a solid – ice. If you heat it, it turns into a gas – water vapour. Your breath contains water vapour. If you breathe onto a very cold window pane, the cold will change the vapour back into tiny drops of water.

**Melting**

**Freezing/Solidifying**

**3**

The particles in this liquid are further apart than the ones in the solid, but they are still able to attract one another. They are not arranged in a regular pattern, and have no shape of their own. The shape of a liquid depends on the container it is in.

**You can break up the particles of a liquid or gas more easily than you can those of a solid, because of the spaces in between.**

**Condensing**

**Evaporating/ Boiling**

**4**

If you heat a liquid, the particles are given even more energy. They move around so much that they eventually escape from the surface of the liquid, and become a gas. Here you can see the particles in a gas. They are moving around very fast, and cannot attract one another much. This is why a gas has no particular shape.

**Why do you think a saucepan overflows when it is boiling?**

57

# Physical changes

When you mix two substances, their particles become jumbled up together. But they do not necessarily combine chemically. Unless the atoms in the molecules are rearranged, the change is only a physical one. The new substance is called a mixture and can usually be separated quite easily.

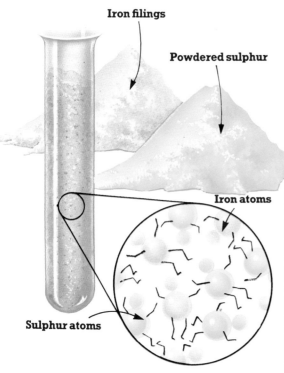

Iron filings

Powdered sulphur

Iron atoms

Sulphur atoms

The properties of substances in a mixture stay the same after they have been mixed. So you can use their properties to try to separate them. Try mixing together iron filings and powdered sulphur*. Iron is a grey metal that sinks in water and is magnetic. Sulphur is a yellow non-metal that floats in water and is not magnetic. Can you think how to separate them? Try out your ideas to see if they work.

## Separating puzzle

How would you separate these things? Tea and sugar, salt and flour, talc and bath salts, a broken jar of pins, a broken bottle of bath salts. Read these two pages first, for clues about which methods to use**.

## Separating things

A lot of chemicals are mixtures of things. If a chemist wants to analyse a substance, the first step is to break it down into elements and compounds. Here are some different ways of separating mixtures. If you know something about the physical properties of the ingredients, it will help you decide which method to use.

A solid dissolved in a liquid is called a solution. You can recover the solid by boiling the solution or leaving it to evaporate.
Lemon juice is a mixture of things, including citric acid and water. To get rid of the water, boil it first, then leave it to evaporate. You will be left with solid crystals.

Lemons

Some metals are magnetic. You can separate them from other substances by using a magnet.

Magnet

An insoluble solid in a liquid is called a suspension. It should separate after being left to stand for a long time. The solid will settle at the bottom.

*You can find out about where to get chemicals on page 92.
**The answers to puzzles are on page 93.

If a mixture contains an insoluble solid and a soluble one, you can separate them by adding water and then pouring it through filter paper. This method can be used to clean up dirty salt. Dissolve the mixture and filter off the dirt. To get back the salt, boil* off most of the water and leave the last bit to evaporate.

**Filter paper**

**Funnel**

**Jug**

**Salt**

Distillation is a way of separating two liquids which have different boilings points. This is used in the manufacture of spirits, such as whisky. Alcohol boils at a lower temperature than water. The mixture is boiled and the alcohol vapour is collected in a test tube, then cooled back into a liquid. Separating it from some of the water makes the alcohol more concentrated. This is why spirits are stronger than beer and wine, which are not distilled.

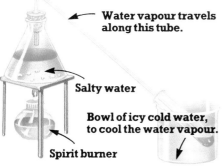

**Water vapour travels along this tube.**

**Salty water**

**Bowl of icy cold water, to cool the water vapour.**

**Spirit burner**

You can use this method to purify salty water. When the water changes into water vapour, it leaves behind the salt and other impurities. The vapour is then cooled to make pure, distilled water.

You can separate the chemicals in inks by a method called chromatography. Take a large piece of blotting paper, filter paper or kitchen towel and put some spots of coloured ink along the bottom. Hang this over a bowl of water, so that the paper just touches the water. As the water is soaked up, it carries the ink with it. Coloured fringes appear as different chemicals in the ink move different distances. This shows you that many inks are made up of different coloured chemicals.

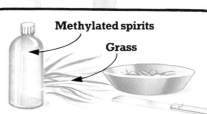

**Methylated spirits**

**Grass**

You can try separating the colours in grass. Chop up some bits of fresh grass in a bowl and crush them with a few drops of methylated spirits. Then do the same test, using water.

*Take care not to boil the pan dry or you may ruin it.

# What is a chemical reaction?

A chemical reaction, or change, occurs when new substances form. This happens when the bonds between atoms or groups of atoms are broken and rearranged to form new compounds. The bonds between them are often strong and this explains why energy, usually in the form of heat, is needed to start a reaction.

## What makes a chemical reaction take place?

When a chemical reaction takes place heat is usually absorbed or given out. Unlike mixtures, compounds have different properties from those of the elements they contain. For example, sodium and chlorine are both dangerous. But they combine with each other to form sodium chloride, which is the salt you eat.

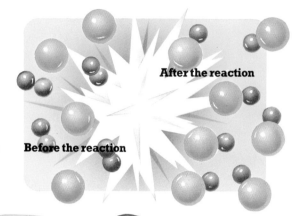

**After the reaction**

**Before the reaction**

If you mix together butter, sugar, flour and baking powder, you get a mixture which still looks, tastes and feels like its ingredients. But when water is added and it is cooked you can see that a chemical reaction has taken place. The baking powder reacts with the other ingredients to give off bubbles of gas (carbon dioxide), which makes the mixture rise. The new substance looks, feels and tastes different from the uncooked mixture and cannot be separated back into the original ingredients.

**These bubbles are made by carbon dioxide gas.**

When you make a cake, it is important to get the quantities right, or the cake may not rise. It is just the same in other chemical reactions.

*You can find out about writing equations on page 90.

# Chemical reactions in your body

The chemical reactions in your body also need energy. They use energy which is produced from eating food and breathing in oxygen. The food and oxygen react together to make water and energy, which you use, and carbon dioxide which you breathe out. You can write this in a word equation.

Carbo-hydrates + oxygen → water + carbon dioxide + energy

## Make a compound

See if you can make a compound from the iron and sulphur mixture you made on page 58. Not all mixtures are capable of forming compounds.

**Mix together six measures of iron to four measures of sulphur and heat them in a test tube. The tube should glow red\* and leave a solid lump. This is the compound iron sulphide.**

Iron and sulphur

**Tongs
(you could use
a wooden
clothes peg)**

**Another test you can do is to put it in some acid. Iron sulphide should produce a gas with a "bad egg" smell.**

Iron sulphide

Iron sulphide
– gas with
"bad egg" smell.

**The compound formed is non-magnetic and sinks in water. So it doesn't behave like iron or sulphur. This is why it is difficult to separate.**
**Sulphur and dilute hydrochloric acid – no reaction.**

Iron and acid
– bubbles, but
no smell.

## Reactions which produce heat

You don't always need heat to set off a chemical reaction. Some reactions produce heat. Try mixing vinegar with bicarbonate of soda. Test the ingredients with a thermometer before and after the reaction. You should see a slight rise in temperature.

## Reactions which use light

Plants use light energy, as well as heat, to carry out chemical reactions inside themselves. Compare this equation with the one for reactions inside your body. It's almost the same reaction in reverse.
**Carbon dioxide + water → sugar + oxygen**

**61**

*Take care! See page 93 for notes on safety.*

# Looking for patterns in chemistry

For centuries chemists have tried to sort chemistry into some sort of order, so as to understand it better. The first step was to identify the building bricks – the elements. By the 19th century, chemists were beginning to find patterns in the behaviour of elements. They found that some reacted often; others hardly at all. By doing lots of experiments they worked out that the atoms of different elements must have different "atomic weights" – now called "relative atomic masses".

A German chemist, Döbereiner, found that bromine, chlorine and iodine reacted similarly. He spotted several other groups and concluded that elements * could be grouped in threes, called triads. An English chemist, Newlands, came closer to the answer. He arranged the elements in order of relative atomic mass and noticed that elements with similar properties occurred at intervals of eight, which he called "octaves".

## The Periodic Table

In 1869 a Russian chemist, Mendeleev, published his Periodic Table. He also arranged the elements in order of relative atomic mass, but he left gaps for elements that he believed had not yet been discovered. This system worked. As new elements have been found over the years, the gaps have been filled. Very few changes in the order of elements in the table have been necessary, even though they are now arranged in order of atomic number** rather than relative atomic mass.

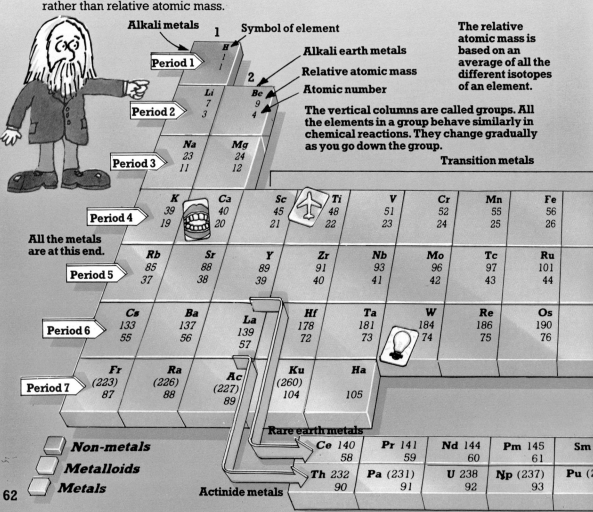

The relative atomic mass is based on an average of all the different isotopes of an element.

The vertical columns are called groups. All the elements in a group behave similarly in chemical reactions. They change gradually as you go down the group.

Non-metals
Metalloids
Metals

62

*You can find a list of elements and their symbols on page 95.
**Atomic number is explained on page 54.

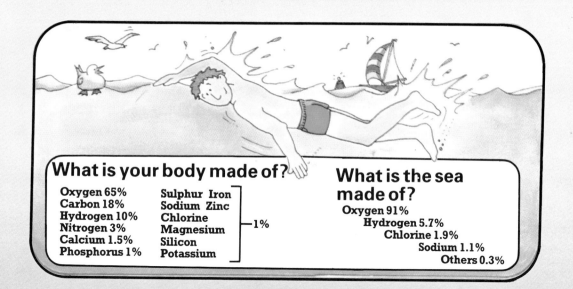

# What is your body made of?

Oxygen 65%
Carbon 18%
Hydrogen 10%
Nitrogen 3%
Calcium 1.5%
Phosphorus 1%

Sulphur Iron
Sodium Zinc
Chlorine
Magnesium
Silicon
Potassium
} 1%

# What is the sea made of?

Oxygen 91%
Hydrogen 5.7%
Chlorine 1.9%
Sodium 1.1%
Others 0.3%

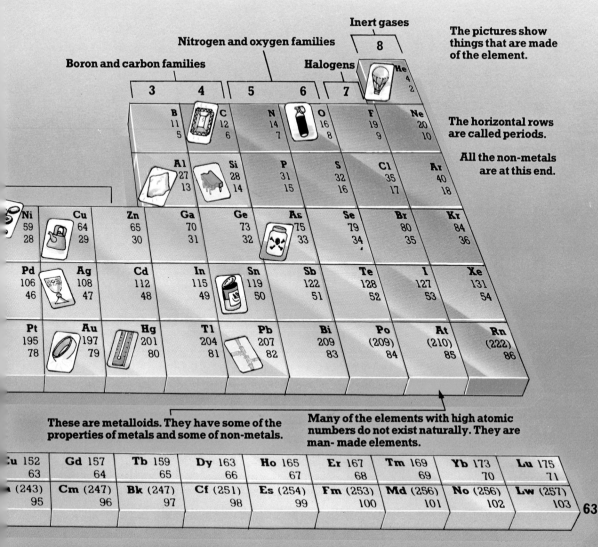

**Inert gases**

**Nitrogen and oxygen families**

**Boron and carbon families**

**Halogens**

The pictures show things that are made of the element.

The horizontal rows are called periods.

All the non-metals are at this end.

|  | 3 | 4 | 5 | 6 | 7 | 8 |
|---|---|---|---|---|---|---|
|  |  |  |  |  |  | He 4 2 |
|  | B 11 5 | C 12 6 | N 14 7 | O 16 8 | F 19 9 | Ne 20 10 |
|  | Al 27 13 | Si 28 14 | P 31 15 | S 32 16 | Cl 35 17 | Ar 40 18 |
| Ni 59 28 | Cu 64 29 | Zn 65 30 | Ga 70 31 | Ge 73 32 | As 75 33 | Se 79 34 | Br 80 35 | Kr 84 36 |
| Pd 106 46 | Ag 108 47 | Cd 112 48 | In 115 49 | Sn 119 50 | Sb 122 51 | Te 128 52 | I 127 53 | Xe 131 54 |
| Pt 195 78 | Au 197 79 | Hg 201 80 | Tl 204 81 | Pb 207 82 | Bi 209 83 | Po (209) 84 | At (210) 85 | Rn (222) 86 |

These are metalloids. They have some of the properties of metals and some of non-metals.

Many of the elements with high atomic numbers do not exist naturally. They are man-made elements.

| Eu 152 63 | Gd 157 64 | Tb 159 65 | Dy 163 66 | Ho 165 67 | Er 167 68 | Tm 169 69 | Yb 173 70 | Lu 175 71 |
|---|---|---|---|---|---|---|---|---|
| Am (243) 95 | Cm (247) 96 | Bk (247) 97 | Cf (251) 98 | Es (254) 99 | Fm (253) 100 | Md (256) 101 | No (256) 102 | Lw (257) 103 |

# Why chemical reactions happen

Looking at an atom's structure can give you clues as to how it will react with other atoms. Scientists believe that the electrons in an atom are arranged in layers, called orbits. There's a limit to the number of electrons that can fit into each orbit. Atoms can have between one and seven orbits. In the Periodic Table, all the elements in a period usually have the same number of orbits. In period 1, they have one orbit, in period 2, they have two orbits, and so on. . .

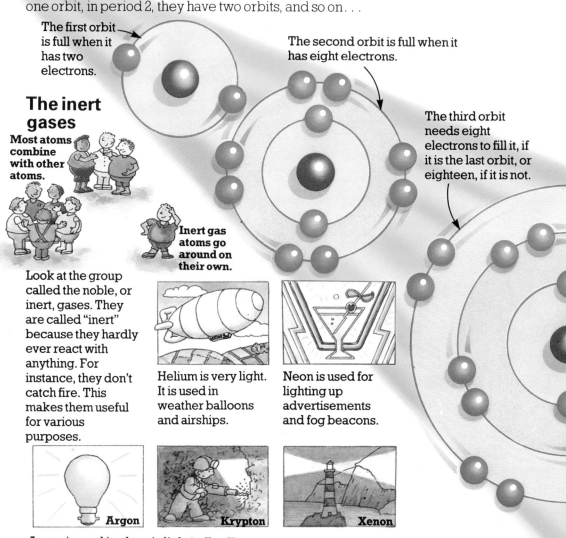

The first orbit is full when it has two electrons.

The second orbit is full when it has eight electrons.

The third orbit needs eight electrons to fill it, if it is the last orbit, or eighteen, if it is not.

## The inert gases

Most atoms combine with other atoms.

Inert gas atoms go around on their own.

Look at the group called the noble, or inert, gases. They are called "inert" because they hardly ever react with anything. For instance, they don't catch fire. This makes them useful for various purposes.

Helium is very light. It is used in weather balloons and airships.

Neon is used for lighting up advertisements and fog beacons.

**Argon**

**Krypton**

**Xenon**

Argon is used in electric light bulbs. Krypton and xenon are used in special bulbs, such as those used in miners' lamps and in lighthouses. Radon is radioactive. It can be used to trace gas leaks and in treating some forms of cancer.

## Why are the inert gases so unreactive?

Why do you think the inert gases are so unreactive? If you look at their structures, you will see that they all have full orbits. That is the clue. Atoms like to have full orbits, with eight in the outer one. In chemical reactions, atoms lose, gain or share electrons in order to end up with full orbits. Atoms with full orbits are very stable, because they don't need to react with other atoms. They already have the right number of electrons.

# What happens in a chemical reaction?

Sodium chloride, or table salt, is a very stable compound. It is made up of sodium, an alkali metal, and chlorine, a halogen, both of which are extremely reactive elements. If you look at the structure of their atoms, you can see why.

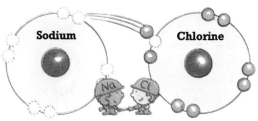

**Sodium has two full orbits, but its outer orbit has only one electron – which it will happily get rid of.**
**Chlorine has seven electrons in its outer orbit. So it needs one more to make it stable.**

**When they react together, chlorine takes the extra electron from sodium. It fills its own orbit and leaves sodium with full orbits too. This way both atoms are satisfied.**

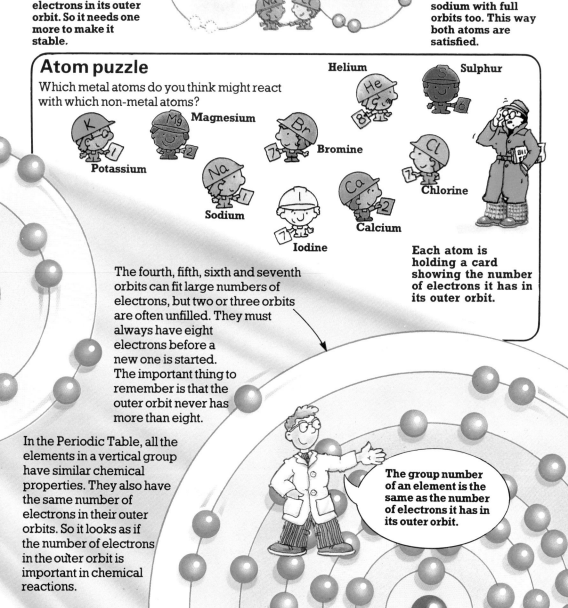

## Atom puzzle

Which metal atoms do you think might react with which non-metal atoms?

Helium

Sulphur

Potassium

Magnesium

Bromine

Sodium

Iodine

Calcium

Chlorine

**Each atom is holding a card showing the number of electrons it has in its outer orbit.**

The fourth, fifth, sixth and seventh orbits can fit large numbers of electrons, but two or three orbits are often unfilled. They must always have eight electrons before a new one is started. The important thing to remember is that the outer orbit never has more than eight.

In the Periodic Table, all the elements in a vertical group have similar chemical properties. They also have the same number of electrons in their outer orbits. So it looks as if the number of electrons in the outer orbit is important in chemical reactions.

**The group number of an element is the same as the number of electrons it has in its outer orbit.**

# Looking at compounds

To understand more about how compounds are formed, you could try testing a few different ones. Here are some experiments you could do with butter, wax, lard, sodium chloride (salt), sodium carbonate (washing powder) and sodium hydrogen carbonate (bicarbonate of soda). Make a chart and write down your results.

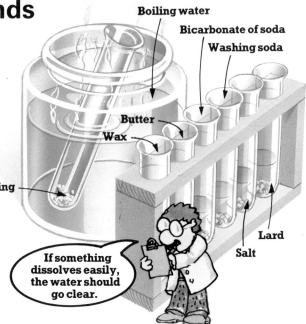

**Boiling water**
**Bicarbonate of soda**
**Washing soda**
**Butter**
**Wax**
**Compound melting**
**Lard**
**Salt**

## Which ones melt easily?

Put a test tube containing each compound into a beaker of boiling water.

## Which ones dissolve easily?

Put a little of each compound into separate test tubes of cold water and stir it. Use enough to cover the end of a spoon handle.

*If something dissolves easily, the water should go clear.*

## Which ones conduct electricity when dissolved in water?

If something conducts electricity, it means it allows electricity to pass through it. Put a little of each compound into separate jars of distilled water.* Set up your apparatus like this. Dip the electrodes into each one. If the bulb lights up, it means that electricity is being conducted.

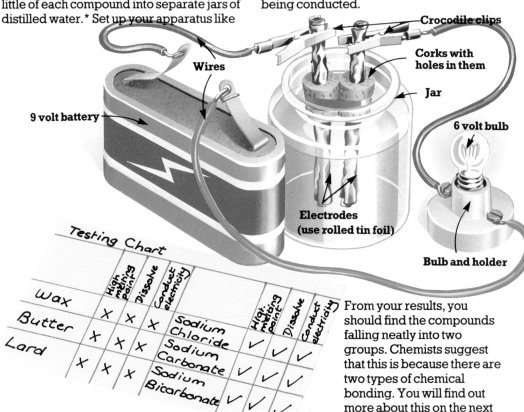

**Crocodile clips**
**Corks with holes in them**
**Wires**
**Jar**
**9 volt battery**
**6 volt bulb**
**Electrodes (use rolled tin foil)**
**Bulb and holder**

### Testing Chart

| | High melting point | Dissolve | Conduct electricity |
|---|---|---|---|
| Wax | X | X | X |
| Butter | X | X | X |
| Lard | X | X | X |

| | High melting point | Dissolve | Conduct electricity |
|---|---|---|---|
| Sodium Chloride | ✓ | ✓ | ✓ |
| Sodium Carbonate | ✓ | ✓ | ✓ |
| Sodium Bicarbonate | ✓ | ✓ | ✓ |

From your results, you should find the compounds falling neatly into two groups. Chemists suggest that this is because there are two types of chemical bonding. You will find out more about this on the next few pages.

66

*You can buy this at the chemist, or at a garage.*

# Looking at your results

One of the groups of compounds all contained sodium. As you know, sodium is highly reactive, because it has one electron that it wants to lose. When it reacts with another element, it loses this electron. This makes it positively charged, because it then has more protons than electrons. An atom that has lost electrons is called a positive ion. Atoms which gain electrons in a reaction are called negative ions. When positive and negative ions join together, an ionic or electrovalent bond is formed. The ions attract each other because of their opposite charges. This makes the bond very strong, and so ionic compounds are difficult to melt. They are always solids.

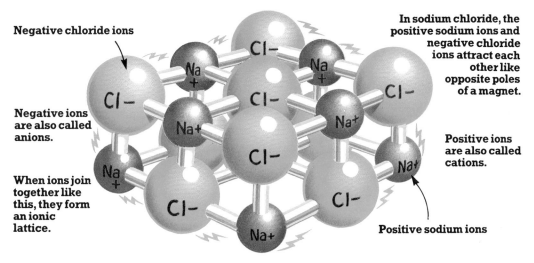

**Negative chloride ions**

**Negative ions are also called anions.**

**When ions join together like this, they form an ionic lattice.**

**In sodium chloride, the positive sodium ions and negative chloride ions attract each other like opposite poles of a magnet.**

**Positive ions are also called cations.**

**Positive sodium ions**

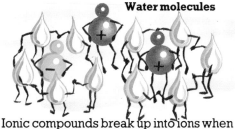

**Water molecules**

Ionic compounds break up into ions when they are in water. This is why they dissolve easily. Water molecules are strongly attracted to ions and can push their way between them.

## Spotting ionic compounds

Ionic compounds are usually made up of a metal and a non-metal. They are made by combining an element which loses electrons easily (on the left of the Periodic Table) with an element which gains electrons easily (on the right of the Periodic Table).

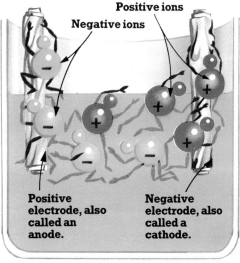

**Positive ions**

**Negative ions**

**Positive electrode, also called an anode.**

**Negative electrode, also called a cathode.**

Ionic compounds are good conductors of electricity, in solution or when molten, because they contain charged particles, or ions. Electric current is a flow of charged particles. When the current is switched on, the negative ions all tend to flow towards the positive electrode, and the positive ions towards the negative electrode. **67**

# Covalent compounds

The other group of compounds in your experiment all contain carbon and hydrogen. If you look at the structure of carbon, you will see that it has four electrons in its outer orbit. This makes it hard to decide whether to lose or gain electrons, in order to fill its orbits. So it doesn't do either. Instead it shares electrons with the atoms of the other elements. When elements share electrons, a covalent compound is formed. Covalent compounds do not conduct heat or electricity, because they do not contain charged particles (ions).

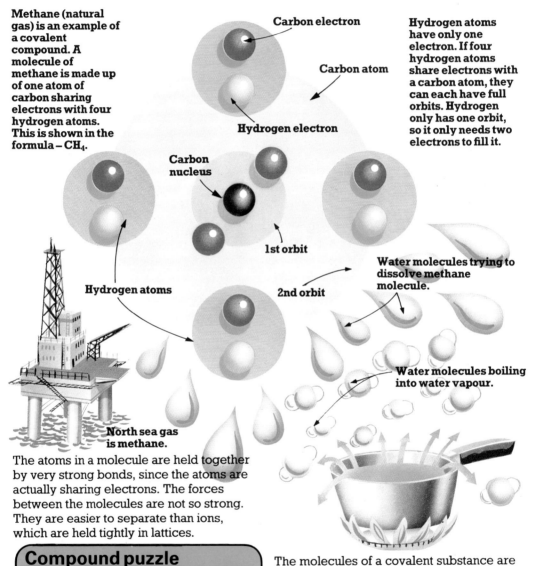

**Methane (natural gas) is an example of a covalent compound. A molecule of methane is made up of one atom of carbon sharing electrons with four hydrogen atoms. This is shown in the formula – CH$_4$.**

Carbon electron

Carbon atom

Hydrogen electron

**Hydrogen atoms have only one electron. If four hydrogen atoms share electrons with a carbon atom, they can each have full orbits. Hydrogen only has one orbit, so it only needs two electrons to fill it.**

Carbon nucleus

1st orbit

2nd orbit

Hydrogen atoms

**Water molecules trying to dissolve methane molecule.**

**Water molecules boiling into water vapour.**

**North sea gas is methane.**

The atoms in a molecule are held together by very strong bonds, since the atoms are actually sharing electrons. The forces between the molecules are not so strong. They are easier to separate than ions, which are held tightly in lattices.

## Compound puzzle

Now that you know about the properties of the two different types of compounds, see if you can work out which group these ones belong to. You could try the same tests as before.

| | |
|---|---|
| Sugar | Methylated spirits |
| Bicycle oil | Epsom salts |

The molecules of a covalent substance are separated when the substance dissolves in a liquid. (Covalent compounds cannot easily dissolve in water, however.) Covalent compounds have low boiling or melting points, because they don't need as much energy (in the form of heat) to push the molecules apart. They are mostly liquids, such as water, or gases.

# Valencies

The number of electrons that an atom needs to gain, lose or share in a chemical reaction is called its valency. The valency of an element is sometimes called its "combining power". Some elements have more than one valency, because they combine in different ways. There is a list of valencies of common elements on page 93. You can guess the valency of an element by looking at its atomic structure.

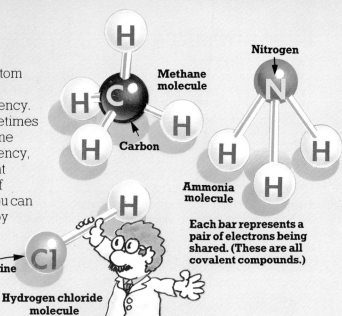

**Methane molecule**

**Carbon**

**Nitrogen**

**Ammonia molecule**

Each bar represents a pair of electrons being shared. (These are all covalent compounds.)

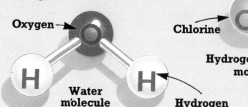

Oxygen →

Chlorine →

**Hydrogen chloride molecule**

**Water molecule**

Hydrogen

Hydrogen has only one electron, and only one to gain, so it must have a valency of one. You can work out the valencies of other elements from the way they combine with hydrogen. For example, in a water molecule, the oxygen atom shares two electrons with the hydrogen atoms. So the valency of oxygen is two.* Using these compounds, see if you can work out the valencies of carbon, nitrogen and chlorine. The valency is the same as the number of bars coming out of each atom.

## Working out formulae from valencies

The proportion of different elements in a compound is shown in its formula. This proportion depends on the valencies of the elements. To form a compound, the total valencies of each element must add up to the same number. If, like chlorine and hydrogen, the elements have the same valency, then they combine in equal proportions. The formula is a simple one, with no numbers in it. If the elements have different valencies, you have to multiply one or both of them, so that they are equal. You can work out the formula of a compound if you know the valencies of its elements.

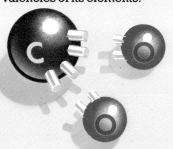

**Carbon: valency 4**
**Oxygen: valency 2**

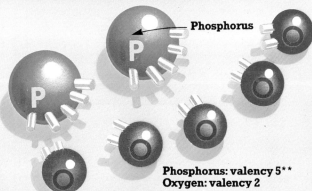

Phosphorus

**Phosphorus: valency 5****
**Oxygen: valency 2**

For example, look at carbon and oxygen. You can make their valencies equal if you multiply oxygen by two. You show this is the formula by writing a small $_2$ after the O. So carbon and oxygen form the compound, carbon dioxide – $CO_2$.

Combining phosphorus and oxygen is more complicated. You have to multiply phosphorus by two and oxygen by five, so that they both add up to ten. They combine to form phosphorus pentoxide, which has the formula $P_2O_5$.

**69**

*You can check this by looking at its atomic structure.
**Phosphorus sometimes has a valency of three.

# Fast and slow reactions

Some chemical reactions take seconds, others take hundreds, or thousands, of years. Caves and potholes are made by a slow chemical reaction. Rain reacts with carbon dioxide in the air, to produce small amounts of weak carbonic acid in the raindrops. When rain falls, it reacts with limestone rocks, wearing them away slowly. Over centuries, it cuts deep grooves in the rock, which eventually form caves.

Fumes from traffic and factory chimneys give off chemicals into the air, which also react with the rain. This produces nitric and sulphuric acid in the rain. These are stronger and much more harmful than carbonic acid. "Acid rain" is killing off forests in some parts of the world.

The acropolis in Athens has been standing for over two thousand years. It is made of marble (another form of calcium carbonate), which has been slowly worn away over the years by wind and rain. This reaction has been speeded up recently by chemical pollution in the atmosphere.

## Speeding up a reaction

Here is an experiment which shows how you can speed up or slow down a reaction. You need to do the same experiment several times, using exactly the same quantities of ingredients each time. Set up your equipment as shown in the picture. The small test tube contains hydrochloric acid. The larger one contains some marble chips.

To start the reaction, you shake the larger tube, so that the ingredients mix. The measuring tube should be full of water when you start. Turn it upside down and put it in a bowl of water, holding something over it as you do so, to stop the water falling out.

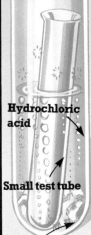

**Cork**

**Large test tube**

**Hydrochloric acid**

**Small test tube**

**Marble chips**

**1**

**Spirit burner**

**Methylated spirits**

Then try the same experiment using acid that has been warmed first. This should make the reaction quicker. The same thing happens to food. It goes bad quite quickly in hot weather. In a freezer you can stop it going bad for months.

**2**

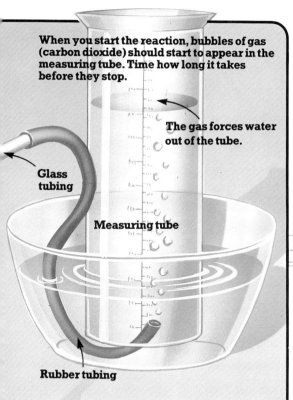

When you start the reaction, bubbles of gas (carbon dioxide) should start to appear in the measuring tube. Time how long it takes before they stop.

The gas forces water out of the tube.

**Glass tubing**

**Measuring tube**

**Rubber tubing**

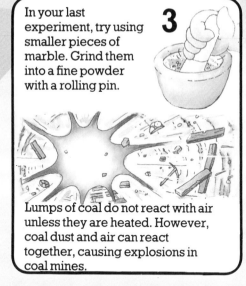

**3**

In your last experiment, try using smaller pieces of marble. Grind them into a fine powder with a rolling pin.

Lumps of coal do not react with air unless they are heated. However, coal dust and air can react together, causing explosions in coal mines.

## Slowing down a reaction

In the next experiment, try diluting the acid with water. This should make the reaction slower. The acid which helps to erode the caves is diluted with a lot of rain. This is why they take so long to form.

## What makes reactions faster?

When you heat something, you give the particles more energy, so they can move faster. They collide more often, and when they do there is more chance of them breaking up and joining in different ways. It's like the difference between a crowd of tortoises (they rarely bump and don't cause much damage) and a stock car race (the cars crash often and do a lot of damage each time).

In the picture below, the red and blue blobs are two different substances. When the large red particle is broken up into smaller ones, more blue particles can cling to it, so the reaction goes faster. In general, smaller pieces of a substance react faster than larger ones.

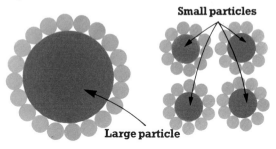

**Small particles**

**Large particle**

The substances which take part in a reaction are called reactants. The more concentrated the reactants are, the faster the reaction will be, because there are more particles available for the reaction. When a substance is diluted, it takes longer for the particles to find each other.

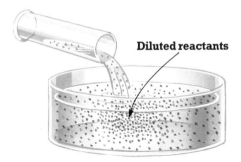

**Diluted reactants**

# Catalysts

A catalyst is something which alters the speed of a reaction, without being permanently changed itself. Some reactions would take years, without the presence of a catalyst.

Here is an experiment you can do using a catalyst. It shows hydrogen peroxide splitting up into oxygen and water. You don't need heat to start this reaction. Hydrogen peroxide reacts when it is exposed to light.

Why do chemists keep hydrogen peroxide in dark bottles?

Set up your equipment as shown in the picture. At the start of the experiment, the test tube should be full of water. Fill it up and keep your thumb over the top as you turn it upside down. There should be enough water in the bowl underneath to cover the opening of the test tube.

As a catalyst, you could use a small piece of liver, or some manganese (IV) oxide (manganese dioxide).* Weigh the catalyst before you start. After the experiment dry it and weigh it again to show that it has not been affected.

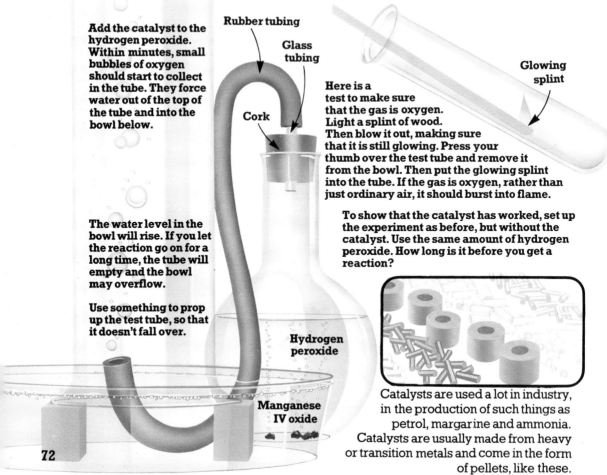

Add the catalyst to the hydrogen peroxide. Within minutes, small bubbles of oxygen should start to collect in the tube. They force water out of the top of the tube and into the bowl below.

The water level in the bowl will rise. If you let the reaction go on for a long time, the tube will empty and the bowl may overflow.

Use something to prop up the test tube, so that it doesn't fall over.

Rubber tubing

Glass tubing

Cork

Here is a test to make sure that the gas is oxygen. Light a splint of wood. Then blow it out, making sure that it is still glowing. Press your thumb over the test tube and remove it from the bowl. Then put the glowing splint into the tube. If the gas is oxygen, rather than just ordinary air, it should burst into flame.

Glowing splint

To show that the catalyst has worked, set up the experiment as before, but without the catalyst. Use the same amount of hydrogen peroxide. How long is it before you get a reaction?

Hydrogen peroxide

Manganese IV oxide

Catalysts are used a lot in industry, in the production of such things as petrol, margarine and ammonia. Catalysts are usually made from heavy or transition metals and come in the form of pellets, like these.

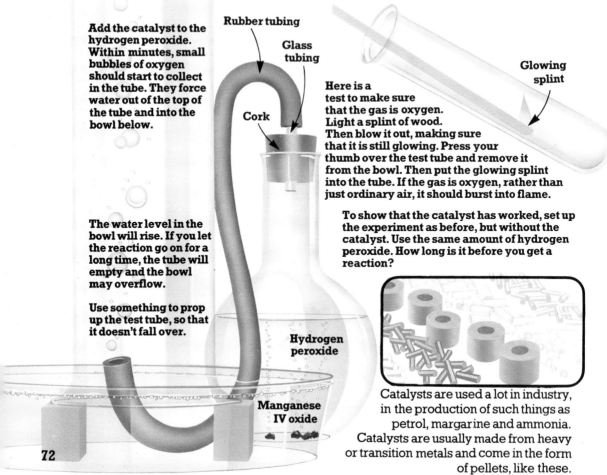

72

*This is one of several compounds made from manganese and oxygen.

# How catalysts work

In order for a reaction to occur, the molecules must have a certain energy called "activation energy". If the activation energy is higher, fewer molecules can react, and the reaction will go slower. A catalyst works by lowering the activation energy. Imagine the activation energy as a hill that you have to ride over – using a catalyst is like taking another path, which avoids the hill.

## Enzymes

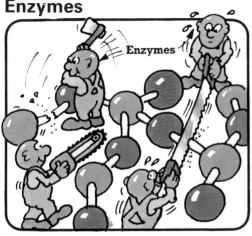

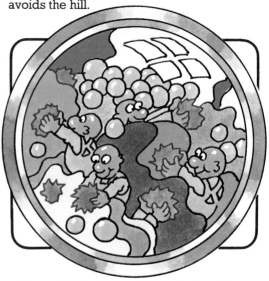

Enzymes are extremely complex chemicals, some of which live in the cells in your body. Amongst other things, they help you digest your food. Enzymes are a sort of catalyst. They often work by breaking bigger molecules into smaller ones. Enzymes are used as catalysts in making cheese, beer, wine, and other things. Biological washing powders contain enzymes which can "eat up" protein stains such as blood. Enzymes are less versatile than other catalysts, so they can only work at certain temperatures.

## Watch an enzyme at work

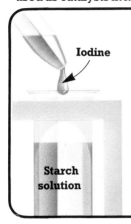

Iodine

Starch solution

If you add iodine to starch, it will go blue. Take two test tubes and put a piece of starch in each (potato or bread). Put some saliva in one of them. Leave them in a warm place for a few days, then test both the tubes with iodine. One goes blue, the other doesn't. What has happened? The answer is that saliva contains an enzyme, called amylase, which breaks down starch into glucose. If you add iodine to glucose, it doesn't go blue.

Starch and saliva mixture

# How metals react

Some metals are highly reactive; others hardly react at all. The very reactive ones are hardly ever found on their own. They form very stable compounds, which are difficult to split. You can find out how reactive a metal is by looking at the activity series, shown below. It lists metals according to how reactive they are with air and water.*

K Na Mg Ca Al Zn Fe Pb Sn Cu Hg Ag Pt Au

**Potassium and sodium are so reactive, they have to be stored in oil – away from contact with the air. In water, potassium catches alight and burns with a pinkish purple flame.**

**Aluminium reacts with air to form a thin, almost invisible coat, which protects it from water. This is why planes are made of aluminium.**

**Zinc reacts very slowly with water. Metals, such as iron, are often coated with zinc – or "galvanized" – to stop rust.**

**Iron rusts.**

**Copper, silver and gold are very unreactive. This is why they are used for jewellery. Tutankhamun's gold mask has survived thousands of years.**

## What makes things rust?

Rust is a common chemical reaction, which happens to iron and metals containing iron. Try this experiment to find out what causes it. You need five test tubes with a little wire wool in each. Then add the following:

1 2 3 4 5

## Oxidation

The activity series can help you understand why some reactions happen.

When an element reacts with oxygen, it produces a compound called an oxide. Chemists call this oxidation. Rust is partly a form of oxidation. Metals lower on the list, such as copper, do not react easily with oxygen. They have to be heated with air to make them react. When a substance burns in oxygen, the reaction is called combustion.

Eating and breathing are also a form of combustion. The food you eat is burnt up inside your body by the oxygen you breathe. This produces energy which you can use.

1. Tap water.

2. Boiled water. (Boiling removes the air bubbles from water. Press the cork right down to stop more air getting in.)

3. Test tube left open, so that air can get in. (Air contains water vapour.)

4. Tap water and salt.

5. Dry air. You can remove water vapour from air by putting a little calcium chloride in the tube, and sealing it.

You will need to leave the tubes for at least a day before you see a reaction. Tube number four should rust first. Rust is caused by a combination of water and air, speeded up by salt. Tubes two and five will only rust if air and water vapour get through the cork into the tube.

74

*You can find the activity series, and a list of elements and their symbols on page 95.

# What is burning?

## Why can nothing burn on the Moon?
(See page 45.)

When a substance burns in air a chemical reaction occurs with the oxygen in the air. This produces light and heat. Burning is a form of oxidation. Most things that burn in air need to be heated to a certain temperature before they will burn.

## Reduction

Reduction is the opposite of oxidation. When something gives oxygen to another substance, chemists say it has been reduced. The other substance has been oxidized. So oxidation and reduction usually happen in the same reaction. Metals high in the series react strongly with oxygen and can remove oxygen from metals lower down the list. This doesn't only apply to removing oxygen. If you add a metal to a solution of a compound containing a less reactive metal, it will "push" the less reactive metal out of the solution.

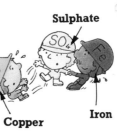

Sulphate

Copper

Iron

Try leaving an iron nail in a solution of copper sulphate. The copper will collect around the nail, turning it pink. This is because the iron has "pushed" the copper out of the solution. Chemists call this a displacement reaction.

## Flame tests

When some metals burn, they produce a distinctive coloured flame. This can help you work out whether a particular metal is present in an unknown compound. You need an unreactive wire, such as nichrome, which will not interfere in the experiment. Dip it in hydrochloric acid to clean it, then heat it red hot. When no colour is added to the flame, dip it in the unknown compound and heat it again.

Calcium

Copper

Sodium

Lithium

Potassium

Barium

Fireworks are made from compounds containing calcium, strontium (crimson) and barium.

# Acids, bases and salts

Acids, bases and salts are three very important groups of chemicals. You can fit most compounds into one or other of these groups. Acids are compounds which produce hydrogen ions when in water. (Remember, ions are atoms which have lost or gained electrons.) Most acids contain oxygen too, as part of an acid radical* ion. Bases are usually metal oxides and hydroxides. Salts are made up of metal ions and acid radical ions. Most compounds ending in -ide, -ite or -ate are salts (except oxides and hydroxides).

All the things on the right contain acids, though some are stronger than others. All acids have a sour taste and strong smell. But never taste chemicals (except foodstuffs such as vinegar). Strong acids burn and sting, and can even dissolve metals.

**Vinegar**

**Car batteries**

**Nettles**

**Lemons**   **Tea leaves**   **Ants**

**Washing soda**

**Oven cleaner**

**Caustic soda**

**Potash**

**Indigestion tablets**

Bases are chemically opposite to acids. Bases that are soluble in water are called alkalis. They have a bitter taste and feel soapy. Strong alkalis burn your skin and can dissolve things. The things on the left all contain alkalis.

## Testing acids and alkalis

You can decide whether something is acid or alkali by using an indicator, such as litmus paper**. Acids turn blue litmus paper red. Alkalis turn red litmus paper blue.

ACID

ALKALI

Chemists use a range of numbers, called pH numbers, to describe how acid or alkaline something is. Acids range from 1 to 6; alkalis from 8 to 14. 7 is neutral. With "universal indicator" papers, the colours change gradually according to the strength of the acid or alkali. (The actual shades vary a little according to the make of indicator.)

1 2 3 4 5 6 7 8 9 10 11 12 13 14

| STRONGLY ACIDIC | WEAKLY ACIDIC | NEUTRAL | WEAKLY ALKALINE | STRONGLY ALKALINE |
| --- | --- | --- | --- | --- |

If you can get some universal indicator, you could try to find the pH numbers of a few different compounds: apple juice, paraffin, toothpaste, salt, sugar, ammonia. (Dissolve any solids in water first.)

76

*A radical is a group of atoms or ions that form part of a molecule or larger ion and behave like a single ion.

# Neutralization

An acid mixed with an alkali produces something called a salt. If you mix the right quantities, they will neutralize one another, and produce a "neutral" salt. Neutral salts do not burn or sting. The salt you eat is one type of salt, but there are many others. You could try making some salt yourself. Pour a little dilute hydrochloric

acid into a jar. Test it with blue litmus paper – which should turn red. Then add dilute sodium hydroxide, a drop at a time. When the litmus turns blue again, add a bit more acid, until the paper turns purple. Then boil away some of the liquid, leaving the rest to evaporate. Then you should be left with salt crystals.

## Other neutralization reactions

If you put lemon juice on your tongue, it will taste sour. Then try adding a pinch of baking powder. It neutralizes the acid, so that it doesn't taste sour any longer.

If you eat too much, a lot of acid is released into your stomach and yout get indigestion. Indigestion tablets contain a mild alkali, which helps to cure it.

You can soothe acid bee stings with bicarbonate of soda, an alkali.

Some plants like an alkaline soil, others, an acid one. Hydrangeas will only produce pink or white flowers in an alkaline soil. If you add a special compound to make the soil more acidic, you will produce blue flowers.

## More reactions with acids

ACID + METAL → SALT + HYDROGEN

Acids react with metals to give off hydrogen, providing the metal is higher in the activity series than hydrogen. The metal is replacing the hydrogen in the acid, because it is more reactive. Pour some hydrochloric acid or vinegar onto some granulated zinc.* Bubbles should appear. Keep your finger over the tube to trap the gas. Then test for hydrogen by inserting a lighted splint. If it is hydrogen, it should burn with a "pop".

ACID + CARBONATE → SALT + CARBON DIOXIDE

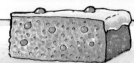

Acids react with carbonates to give off carbon dioxide. You may have seen this happening if you did the experiment on page 70. A similar sort of reaction happens inside a cake. Baking powder contains tartaric acid and sodium hydrogen carbonate. When they are heated they react together to produce bubbles of carbon dioxide inside the cake.

77

*Always add the acid to the other chemical, not the other way around.*

# What is organic chemistry?

Organic chemistry is the study of compounds containing carbon.* It is called "organic", because chemists used to think that these compounds could only be found in living organisms. All living things do contain carbon, but so do plastics, medicines, artifical fabrics and many other man-made substances. So it is really just a convenient way of dividing up chemistry.

Carbon compounds are often made up of very large, sometimes giant, molecules, containing hundreds, or even thousands, of atoms. This is because carbon atoms form very

stable, covalent bonds with other atoms, and can link themselves into long chains and rings. Organic compounds usually contain only a few other elements – such as hydrogen and oxygen. But there are so many different possible combinations, that they can form a great variety of different compounds.

## Testing organic compounds

All foods are organic compounds. When they are burnt they often go black – like coal, which is a form of carbon. They give off carbon dioxide.

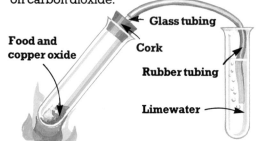

**Glass tubing**

**Food and copper oxide**

**Cork**

**Rubber tubing**

**Limewater**

Carbon dioxide turns limewater milky. So test this by bubbling it through limewater. To make the limewater, dissolve some calcium hydroxide in water. Some of it will settle on the bottom. Then pour the top, clear liquid into a test tube.

The same thing happens when you eat. There is a lot of organic chemistry going on inside you. Your body burns the food and you breathe out carbon dioxide. Blow through a straw into the limewater.** What happens?

## Digestion

Food is mostly made up of huge molecules of carbohydrates, proteins and fats. These are broken down into much smaller molecules by digestion. Digestion is carried out with the help of organic catalysts, called enzymes, in the mouth, stomach and digestive tract. Here are examples of a few of the different enzymes.

**This is a starch molecule. A lot of foods contain starch – bread, potatoes, cakes, vegetables. It is made up of smaller molecules of glucose, linked together.**

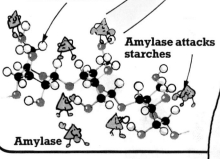

**Starch molecule**

**Amylase attacks starches**

**Amylase**

*A few simple compounds, such as carbon dioxide, are not counted as organic.
**Make sure you don't breathe in!

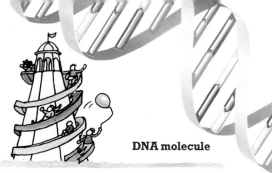

DNA molecule

## DNA

One very interesting organic compound is DNA (deoxyribonucleic acid), a substance which is found in all living cells. In 1954, in Cambridge, two scientists, Francis Crick and James Watson, worked out the structure of its molecules. Each one is shaped in a double helix – rather like two helter skelters wound round each other.

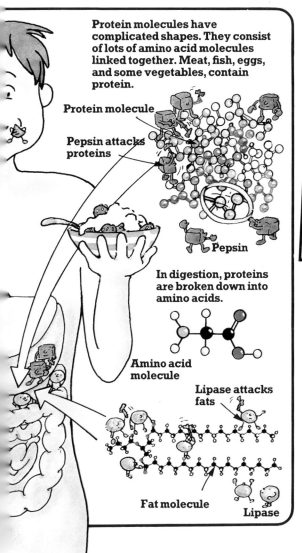

Protein molecules have complicated shapes. They consist of lots of amino acid molecules linked together. Meat, fish, eggs, and some vegetables, contain protein.

Protein molecule

Pepsin attacks proteins

Pepsin

In digestion, proteins are broken down into amino acids.

Amino acid molecule

Lipase attacks fats

Fat molecule

Lipase

# Fermentation

Fermentation is a way of breaking down carbohydrates by means of enzymes produced by a fungus called yeast. Fermentation produces alcohol. There are many different types of alcohol. The type found in drinks is called ethanol.

## Making wine

You could try fermenting some fruit juice. Mix together a carton of fruit juice, about 200g of sugar, a pinch of yeast and some water.

Put it in a corked container. Insert a glass tube in the top, with the end in a jar of limewater. This allows carbon dioxide to escape, without letting oxygen in.

Leave in a warm place for a few days. You should see the limewater going milky, showing that carbon dioxide has been given off. You will need to leave it for a few weeks before it ferments properly.

Alcohols react with oxygen to produce organic acids. If you leave a bottle of wine open for a few days, it will become oxidized by the air. The result is ethanoic acid, which tastes sour. This is the acid you get in vinegar.

VINO

# Organic families

Organic compounds can be divided into well-defined groups and families. The simplest of these groups is the hydrocarbons. The hydrocarbons are divided into families, such as the alkanes, with similar chemical properties. Their properties change gradually according to the size of the molecule.

## Alkanes

Here are the first six members of the alkane family. It starts with methane, which is the simplest organic compound. The alkanes increase in size in a regular pattern.* Alkanes are fairly unreactive because they are what chemists call saturated compounds – they contain only single covalent bonds. From pentane onwards, the first part of the name tells you how many carbon atoms the molecule has.**

**Alkanes with less than four carbons are gases. Between five and 16, they are liquids, such as petrol. With more than 16 carbons, they are solids, such as candle wax.**

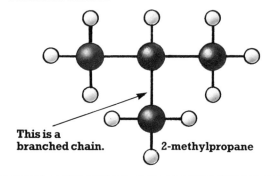

| Name | Formula | Boiling point °C | Uses |
|------|---------|------------------|------|
| Methane | $CH_4$ | −162°C |  |
| Ethane | $C_2H_6$ | −89°C | Natural gas |
| Propane | $C_3H_8$ | −4°C | Camping gaz |
| Butane | $C_4H_{10}$ | −1°C |  |
| Pentane | $C_5H_{12}$ | +36°C |  |
| Hexane | $C_6H_{14}$ | +69°C | Petrol |

These are called unbranched chains.

## Isomers

Isomers are compounds which have the same formula as each other, but different structures. So they have the same number of atoms of each element, but they are arranged in different ways. Butane and 2-methylpropane are isomers. Unlike butane, 2-methylpropane has a branched chain structure. Count up the atoms, and you will see that there are just as many carbons and hydrogens as in butane. But the difference in structure makes them behave differently.

This is a branched chain.

2-methylpropane

## Make a molecular model

Chemists often build molecular models, to help them see what might happen in a chemical reaction. This is very important when you are dealing with complicated molecules. They are very difficult to draw two-dimensionally on paper. You could try to make a model of ethanol. You need matches and some plasticine. Make two large black balls, six small white ones and a red one.

Take one of the black balls (carbon) and stick four matches into it – in the shape of a tetrahedron.

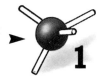

Repeat this with the other one, then remove one of the sticks. Join the two carbon atoms together, using the hole you have just made.

Attach white balls (hydrogens) to the ends of five of the sticks, and a red one (oxygen) to the sixth one.

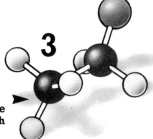

80

*This is expressed in the formula $C_nH_2n+2$.

**Each name is based on the Greek word for the number: pente = 5, hex = 6, etc.

## Alkenes

The alkenes are another family of hydrocarbons. They have two fewer hydrogen atoms in each molecule than each equivalent alkane. Alkenes are said to be unsaturated, because they contain double bonds. This means that the carbon atoms share two pairs of electrons with each other. Alkenes are fairly reactive, because of this "spare" bond, which could be joined to other atoms.

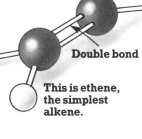

**Double bond**

This is ethene, the simplest alkene.

## Polymers

Polymers are giant molecules, made by linking lots of smaller, identical molecules together. These smaller molecules are called monomers. They contain double or triple bonds, which are removed when the molecules become linked to each other. This is called polymerization. A lot of polymers come from natural substances, such as cellulose, which is found in plants

**Polyethene molecules contain up to 50,000 atoms.**

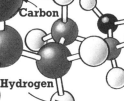

**Carbon**

**Hydrogen**

This is polyethene, another name for the plastic, polythene. It is made by adding lots of ethene molecules together.

Polymer comes from the Greek, meaning "many parts".

## Alkynes

Alkynes are even more reactive than alkenes. They have four fewer hydrogen atoms than they need in each molecule. So the carbon atoms have to share three pairs of electrons. This is called a triple bond.

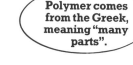

**Triple bond**

To complete the model, put another stick in the oxygen atom, and put a hydrogen on the end.

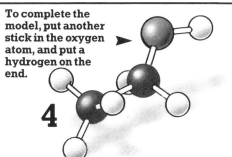

**4**

See if you can make an isomer of ethanol. Take your model apart and join up all the atoms in a different way, using all the same holes. Find the answer on page 93.

## Cyclic hydrocarbons

A few hydrocarbons, such as benzene, contain atoms held in rings. This structure was discovered by a 19th-century German chemist, called Kekulé. Some people at the time made fun of the idea by drawing a ring made up of six monkeys. They joined hands to form single bonds, and tails to form double bonds.

**Benzene**

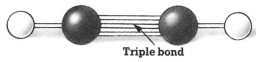

# Useful organic compounds

## Crude oil

Crude oil contains lots of alkanes, which have different boiling points. It can be separated into many useful chemical products in a process called fractional distillation. The oil is heated and the products, known as fractions, are collected at different temperatures.

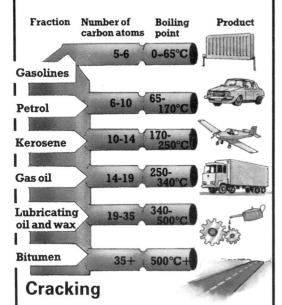

| Fraction | Number of carbon atoms | Boiling point | Product |
|---|---|---|---|
| Gasolines | 5-6 | 0-65°C | |
| Petrol | 6-10 | 65-170°C | |
| Kerosene | 10-14 | 170-250°C | |
| Gas oil | 14-19 | 250-340°C | |
| Lubricating oil and wax | 19-35 | 340-500°C | |
| Bitumen | 35+ | 500°C+ | |

## Cracking

Many of the useful alkanes, such as petrol, are made up of small molecules with low boiling points. Crude oil contains a lot of alkanes with larger molecules and high boiling points. There isn't enough of the fraction containing petrol to satisfy world demand. However, chemists have found a way of breaking these heavier alkanes into shorter, lighter ones. It is done by heating them to very high temperatures with a catalyst. This process is called cracking.

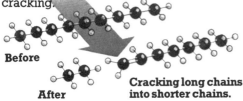

Before

After

Cracking long chains into shorter chains.

An important ingredient of petrol is 2,2,4-trimethyl pentane (once called iso-octane). The "octane" rating is used as a way of grading petrol. The higher the octane number, the better the petrol.

## Plastics

Plastics are a group of polymers which are mostly man-made. They have qualities that are extremely useful. They are strong, easy to colour and clean. They keep in warmth and insulate against electricity. They do not usually rot or wear away.

There are two main types of plastics – thermoplastics and thermosets. Thermoplastics include polyethene, PVC, nylon and polystyrene. They are made up of molecules linked together in unbranched chains. They can be heated, moulded and hardened over and over again.

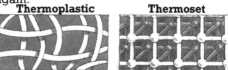

Thermoplastic          Thermoset

Thermosets do not melt. Their molecules are linked in chains and set hard. They cannot be remoulded. Formica and bakelite (the first plastic, invented in 1933), are thermosets.

## Make your own plastic

You can make a type of plastic by boiling milk with vinegar. A white, elastic substance is formed.

## Identifying plastics

| TEST for ... | PVC | POLY STYRENE | POLY THENE |
|---|---|---|---|
| Does it break/cut easily? | With scissors | Breaks when hit with a hammer | With scissors |
| Does it bend easily? | Usually does | Usually doesn't | Some bend easily, others dont |
| Does it float? | No | Yes | Yes |
| Is it softened by heat? | Yes | Yes | Yes |
| How does it burn? | With difficulty. Produces white, acrid fumes and a yellow flame. Does not burn long. | Easily. Produces sooty smoke with a flowery smell and a deep yellow flame. Continues to burn. | Easily. Produces a yellow/blue flame and little smoke. Smells waxy and continues to burn. |

BEWARE FUMES!

# Fats and margarines

Animal fats and vegetable oils belong to a group of compounds called esters. Esters are made by mixing an organic acid with an alcohol. Fats can be solid or liquid. They are insoluble in water, but soluble in many organic solvents, such as dry-cleaning fluid. They float, as they are less dense than water.

## What are polyunsaturates?

Some margarines are advertised as having polyunsaturated fats. This means the molecules contain many (poly) double or triple bonds, because they do not have enough hydrogen. Polyunsaturated fats are supposed to be healthier and reduce the risk of heart disease. They are almost liquid at room temperature and spread like butter. Adding hydrogen, to reduce the double bonds, makes them solid but saturated.

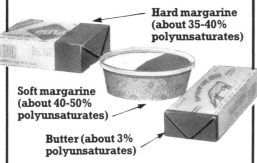

Hard margarine (about 35-40% polyunsaturates)

Soft margarine (about 40-50% polyunsaturates)

Butter (about 3% polyunsaturates)

You can test butter and margarine by using iodine and an organic solvent.

Butter

hard margarine

Iodine

Soft margarine

Add some iodine to each test tube, drop by drop. The unsaturated molecules will react with iodine and absorb the colour. When the colour reappears, it means that the solution is saturated. Count how many drops it takes for this to happen.

# What is soap?

Soap is really a kind of salt. It is a sodium or potassium salt, made by combining an organic acid with an alkali.

## How soap works

Water often seems to have a sort of skin which allows things to float on it. This is called surface tension. It happens because water molecules are very strongly attracted to one another. Water and oil do not mix, so water isn't attracted to molecules of greasy dirt. Soaps and detergents work by lowering the surface tension, so that the water will spread more easily over the things you want to wash.

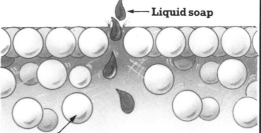

◄— Liquid soap

Water molecules

Soap molecules are made up of two parts – a long hydrocarbon tail, which repels water, and a head made up of charged ions, which attracts water. By attracting water, the ions reduce the attraction water molecules have for each other.

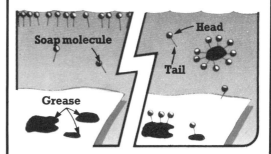

Soap molecule

Head

Tail

Grease

The hydrocarbon tail is attracted to the dirt and grease in the clothes. The tail sticks into the dirt, and at the same time, the water-loving head pulls away from the clothes towards the water. This pulls the grease out of the clothes.

# Splitting compounds

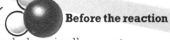

Although the elements in a compound are bonded chemically, most compounds can be split by some means or another. A reaction in which a compound breaks down into simpler molecules is called a decompositon reaction. You will already have come across examples of these earlier in this section. All replacement reactions, such as the one with copper sulphate and iron*, involve the splitting of a compound.

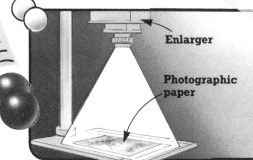

**Enlarger**

**Photographic paper**

To split a compound, you nearly always need some kind of energy. A few compounds will split up after being exposed to light. Silver bromide, for example, is used in the production of photographic paper and film because of its sensitivity to light. Some compounds will split up after being heated. Mercury oxide, for example, decomposes to form mercury and oxygen when you heat it.

**After the reaction**

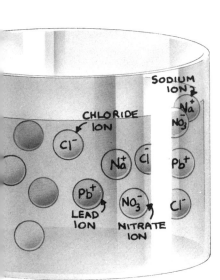

SODIUM ION

CHLORIDE ION

Na⁺

NO₃⁻

Cl⁻

Na⁺  Cl  Pb⁺

Pb⁺  NO₃⁻  Cl⁻

LEAD ION    NITRATE ION

## Double decomposition

Double decomposition is when two compounds split up and swap partners. Most salts are soluble in water, but some are not. When you dissolve salts in water, they split up into separate ions. If two salts swap their partner ions, an insoluble salt may be produced. The insoluble salt forms a "precipitate", a solid which settles at the bottom. This is also called a precipitation reaction. Sodium chloride and lead nitrate are both soluble salts. When you dissolve them together, they swap partners and lead chloride forms a precipitate.

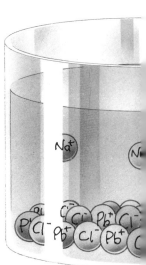

---

### SOLUBILITY GUIDE

* ALL NITRATES ARE SOLUBLE.

* ALL POTASSIUM, SODIUM AND AMMONIUM SALTS ARE SOLUBLE IN WATER.

If sodium carbonate and zinc sulphate are dissolved in water and swap partners, which one will be the precipitate? Use this chart. It shows which salts are soluble and which are not.

* ALL CARBONATES ARE INSOLUBLE, EXCEPT SODIUM, POTASSIUM AND AMMONIUM.

* ALL SULPHATES ARE SOLUBLE IN WATER EXCEPT BARIUM, LEAD, SILVER AND CALCIUM.

* ALL CHLORIDES ARE SOLUBLE, EXCEPT SILVER AND LEAD.

* ALL BROMIDES ARE SOLUBLE, EXCEPT SILVER AND LEAD.

*You can find this reaction on page 75.

# Electrolysis

The most reactive elements require a great deal of energy to release them from their compounds. One method is to pass electricity through them. This is called electrolysis. Substances that allow electricity to pass through them are called electrolytes. All ionic compounds are electrolytes, when molten*, or in solution.

## How electrolysis works

When the electricity is switched on, current flows through the circuit. In the wires, the current is carried by electrons, which move from the negative to the positive terminal. In the liquid, the current is carried by the ions of the compound. The negative ions travel towards the positive electrode, and the positive ions towards the negative electrode. This is because the ions are attracted by opposite charges. At the electrodes, the positive ions receive electrons and the negative ions lose electrons. This way, they are both turned back into "neutral" atoms.

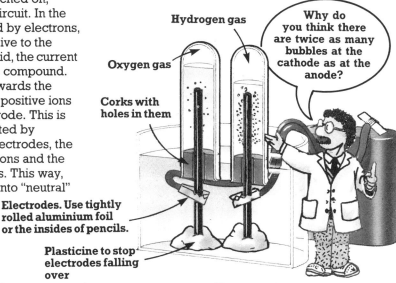

Hydrogen gas

Oxygen gas

Corks with holes in them

**Why do you think there are twice as many bubbles at the cathode as at the anode?**

Electrodes. Use tightly rolled aluminium foil or the insides of pencils.

Plasticine to stop electrodes falling over

## Splitting water

Water contains positive hydrogen ions and negative oxygen ions. You can split water by using electrolysis. When you put the electrodes in the water, bubbles will start to appear around them. You can test these gases by putting a glowing piece of wood at the bottom of the tube. Remember, oxygen will relight it; hydrogen makes it go "pop".

## Using electrolysis

Electrolysis has many uses in industry. It is used for extracting highly reactive metals from their compounds. It is also used for plating things with another metal. This is how silver-plated cutlery is made. The knife or fork is put at the cathode, while a silver compound is electrolysed. The silver ions flow towards the cathode, coating the knife with silver.

## Electrolysis and the activity series

If a mixture of compounds is electrolysed, the ions of the least reactive elements will be turned back into atoms first. This is because they don't need as much energy to split them from their compounds. If you electrolyse a compound in water, the metal will only be deposited at the cathode if it is lower than hydrogen** in the activity series. If not, hydrogen ions from the water will be deposited there instead. All salts of highly reactive metals, such as sodium, have to be electrolysed in a molten state.

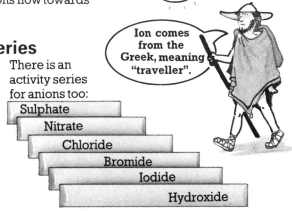

There is an activity series for anions too:

**Ion comes from the Greek, meaning "traveller".**

Sulphate
Nitrate
Chloride
Bromide
Iodide
Hydroxide

The ones at the bottom of the list will be deposited at the anode first.

---

*Molten means melted.   **Hydrogen is not a metal, but it is included in the activity series.     85

# Identifying substances

Here are some clues to help you guess the identity of an unknown substance. You could try out these tests on a chemical from a chemistry set. There isn't room to include all the tests that chemists do, but these ones will help you identify quite a few common chemicals. You can find the instructions for most of these tests explained earlier in this section of the book. If you can't remember how to do them, you could look them up, under "tests", in the index.

Try separating your substance first to make sure it isn't a mixture. Use at least three of the tests shown on pages 10-11.

If it separates into several substances, try these tests on each substance.

It's iron, or a metal containing iron.

Do the flame test to find the metal.

**NO RESULT?**

Is it magnetic?

YES

NO

## Flame tests

| FLAME | CONTAINS |
|-------|----------|
| Blue | Caesium |
| Green | Copper |
| Lilac | Potassium |
| Red/Pink | Lithium |
| Yellow | Sodium |
| Apple green | Barium |
| Crimson | Strontium |
| Brick red | Calcium |

Is it a metal? Does it conduct heat or electricity?

YES

NO

It's probably copper oxide

It's probably carbon.

Which metal does it contain? Do the flame test.

Find out which acid radical it contains.

Heat it. Is carbon dioxide given off?

YES

NO

It's an insoluble salt. Look up the solubility guide.*

It's a non-metal. Does it melt easily?

YES

NO

It's probably an ionic compound.

Is it a black powder?

YES

NO

It's a covalent compound or an element.

Is it a purplish black solid?

Is it none of these?

Does it dissolve easily?

NO

YES

Is it a yellow powder?

Is it a reddish yellow solid?

YES

YES

It could be iodine.

It is organic. It contains carbon.

It could be sulphur.

It could be phosphorus.

Then it's possibly an organic compound.

Heat it. Is carbon dioxide given off?

YES

*See page 83.

# Borax bead test

Heat a loop of platinum wire ** and then dip it in distilled water. Dip it in sodium borate and heat the wire until you get a glass-like "bead". Add a bit of the unknown substance and heat it again. Substances containing certain metals produce different coloured beads. The colours depend on whether you have heated it on the inside or outside part of the flame.

No result? Try the Borax bead test.

| INSIDE FLAME | OUTSIDE FLAME | Contains |
|---|---|---|
| | Blue | Chromium |
| | Green | Cobalt |
| Red/Brown | Turquoise | Copper |
| Dark green | Yellow | Iron |
| Pale green | Purple | Manganese |
| Black | Red/Brown | Nickel |

It's sulphuric acid.

The acid radical is sulphate.

**YES** — Does it give a white precipitate when added to barium chloride?

The acid radical is chloride.

**YES** — Does it give a white precipitate when added to silver nitrate?

It's hydrochloric acid.

It's carbonic acid or a carbonate.

The acid radical is carbonate.

Does it give off carbon dioxide when heated.

Find out which metal it contains. Do the flame tests.

Combine the metal and the acid radical to get the name of the compound.*

Which acid radical does it contain? Do the acid radical tests.

It's an acid! Which one? Do the ACID RADICAL TESTS.

It's an acidic salt.

**YES** — It's acidic. Is it an acid or an acidic salt. Heat it with zinc. Does it give off hydrogen?

**NO**

Do the flame tests to find the metal. Then combine it with the acid radical, or oxide, or hydroxide, to work out the name of the compound.*

It's alkaline. It's probably an oxide or hydroxide of a metal

If it doesn't contain one of these radicals, it may be an oxide or hydroxide.

**ACIDIC** — Is it acidic, alkaline or neutral? Use an indicator to find out.

**ALKALINE**

Does it smell of ammonia?

**YES** — It's an ammonium compound.

**NO** — Do the acid radical tests.

**NEUTRAL**

It's a neutral salt.

Which metal does it contain? Do the flame tests.

Which acid radical does it contain? Do the acid radical tests.

Combine the metal and the acid radical to find the name of the compound.*

*The metal always comes first.

**You need a bunsen burner for this experiment.

87

# Computer program

If you have a microcomputer, or can borrow one, you could use it to try out the tests for identifying an unknown substance. This program is written to work on a BBC microcomputer. Lines that need changing for other computers are marked with a symbol and printed at the end of the program. Each symbol corresponds to a different computer. They are:

▲ VIC and PET
▮ ZX SPECTRUM
● APPLE
○ ORIC
■ ZX SPECTRUM, DRAGON and TRS- 80

```
 10 REM * IDENTIFYING SUBSTANCES *
 20 REM * --------------------- *
 30 GOSUB 930
 40 GOSUB 830
 50 LET N=1
●▲ 60 CLS
 70 REM * MAIN LOOP *
 80 PRINT
 90 PRINT Q$(N);
100 LET F=A(N,1)
110 IF F=0 THEN GOSUB 230
120 IF F=1 THEN GOSUB 310
130 IF N<>0 THEN GOTO 80
140 REM * END PAGE *
150 PRINT
160 PRINT "THATS AS FAR AS WE CAN GO"
170 PRINT "DO YOU WANT TO RUN "
180 PRINT "THE PROGRAM AGAIN? (Y/N)"
190 INPUT A$
200 IF A$="Y" THEN GOTO 40
210 PRINT "O.K "
220 STOP
230 REM * PRINT A STATEMENT *
240 PRINT:PRINT
250 GOSUB 690
260 LET P=A(N,2)
270 IF P=1 THEN GOSUB 360
280 IF P=2 THEN GOSUB 590
290 LET N=A(N,3)
300 RETURN
```

```
310 REM * ASK A QUESTION *
320 PRINT " ?":PRINT
330 GOSUB 740
340 LET N=A(N,R+1)
▲● 350 CLS:RETURN
360 REM * FLAME TEST *
▲● 370 CLS:PRINT
380 PRINT "FLAME TESTS"
390 PRINT
400 PRINT "REFER TO PAGE 75 OF"
410 PRINT "THE BOOK FOR THE "
420 PRINT "DETAILS OF THIS TEST"
430 PRINT
440 PRINT "DO YOU HAVE A RESULT?"
450 GOSUB 740
460 IF R=2 THEN GOSUB 480
470 RETURN
480 REM * BORAX TEST *
▲● 490 CLS:PRINT
500 PRINT "BORAX BEAD TEST"
510 PRINT
520 PRINT "REFER TO PAGES 86-87"
530 PRINT "OF THE BOOK FOR THE "
540 PRINT "DETAILS OF THIS TEST"
550 PRINT
560 GOSUB 690
▲● 570 CLS
580 RETURN
590 REM * ACID TEST *
▲● 600 CLS:PRINT
610 PRINT "ACID RADICAL TEST":PRINT
620 PRINT
630 PRINT "REFER TO PAGES 86-87"
640 PRINT "OF THE BOOK FOR THE "
650 PRINT "DETAILS OF THIS TEST"
660 PRINT
670 GOSUB 690
680 RETURN
690 REM * KEY PRESS *
● 700 PRINT "PRESS SPACE TO CONTINUE"
■▲●○ 710 LET A$=INKEY$(0)
720 IF A$<>" " THEN GOTO 710
730 RETURN
740 REM * GET Y/N ANSWER *
750 PRINT
760 LET R=0
770 PRINT "ANSWER Y/N"
780 INPUT A$
790 IF A$="Y" THEN LET R=1
```

```
         800 IF A$="N" THEN LET R=2
         810 IF R=0 THEN GOTO 780
         820 RETURN
         830 REM * INTRO PAGE *
▲●840 CLS:PRINT
         850 PRINT "IDENTIFYING SUBSTANCES"
         860 PRINT "---------------------"
         870 PRINT
         880 PRINT "TRY THESE TESTS ON"
         890 PRINT "EACH SUBSTANCE."
         900 PRINT
         910 GOSUB 690
         920 CLS:RETURN
         930 REM * READ IN THE DATA *
■940 DIM Q$(54),A(54,3)
         950 LET K=1
         960 READ A$
  970 IF A$="END OF DATA" THEN RETURN
  980 LET Q$(K)=A$
  990 FOR I=1 TO 3
1000 READ A(K,I)
1010 NEXT I
1020 LET K=K+1
1030 GOTO 960
1040 REM * THE DATA *
1050 DATA "DOES IT CONDUCT HEAT OR ELECTRIC
ITY",1,2,5,"IT'S A METAL. IS IT MAGNETIC",1,
3,4
1060 DATA "IT IS, OR CONTAINS IRON",0,0,0,"
TRY FLAME TESTS",0,1,0
1070 DATA "DOES IT MELT EASILY",1,6,17,
"IT'S A COVALENT COMPOUND OR ELEMENT",0,0,7
1080 DATA "IS IT A YELLOW POWDER",1,10,8,
"OR A RED/YELLOW SOLID",1,11,9
1090 DATA "OR A PURPLE/BLACK SOLID",1,12,13
,"IT'S PROBABLY SULPHUR",0,0,0
1100 DATA "IT'S PROBABLY PHOSPHOROUS",0,0,0
,"IT'S PROBABLY IODINE",0,0,0
1110 DATA "IT COULD BE AN ORGANIC COMPOUND"
,0,0,14,"HEAT IT. IS CARBON DIOXIDE GIVEN OFF"
,1,16,15
1120 DATA "IT'S NOT ORGANIC",0,0,0,"IT'S
ORGANIC AND CONTAINS CARBON",0,0,0
1130 DATA "IT'S PROBABLY AN IONIC COMPOUND"
,0,0,18,"DOES IT DISSOLVE",1,24,19
1140 DATA "IS IT A BLACK POWDER",1,20,23,
"HEAT IT. IS CARBON DIOXIDE GIVEN OFF",1,21,22
1150 DATA "IT'S CARBON",0,0,0,"IT'S COPPER
OXIDE",0,0,0
```

```
1160 DATA "IT'S AN INSOLUBLE SALT",0,0,29,"
FIND PH RATING",0,0,25
1170 DATA "IS IT AN ACID",1,42,26,"IS IT AN
ALKALI",1,33,27
1180 DATA "IS IT NEUTRAL",1,28,25,"IT'S A
NEUTRAL SALT",0,0,29
1190 DATA "FIND METAL CONTAINED",0,1,30,
"FIND THE ACID CONTAINED",0,2,31
1200 DATA "COMBINE THE METAL AND THE ACID
RADICAL",0,0,32,"TO FIND THE COMPOUND NAME",0
,0,0
1210 DATA "IT COULD BE AN OXIDE OR...",0,0,
34,"HYDROXIDE OF A METAL",0,0,35
1220 DATA "DOES IT SMELL OF AMMONIA",1,54,3
6,"DO ACID RADICAL TEST",0,2,37
1230 DATA "DO YOU HAVE A RESULT",1,39,38,
"IT'S PROBABLY AN OXIDE OR HYDROXIDE",0,0,39
1240 DATA "FIND THE METAL CONTAINED",0,1,40
,"COMBINE WITH THE ACID RADICAL",0,0,41
1250 DATA "OR OXIDE OR HYDROXIDE FOR
COMPOUND",0,0,0,"ADD ZINC. IS HYDROGEN
GIVEN OFF", 1,44,43
1260 DATA "IT'S AN ACID SALT",0,0,29,"IT'S
AN ACID",0,0,45
1270 DATA "DO ACID RADICAL TEST",0,2,46,"IS
THE RADICAL SULPHATE",1,49,47
1280 DATA "OR CHLORIDE",1,50,48,"OR
CARBONATE",1,51,52
1290 DATA "IT'S SULPHURIC ACID",0,0,0,"IT'S
HYDROCHLORIC ACID",0,0,0
1300 DATA "IT'S CARBONIC ACID",0,0,0,"IT
COULD BE A NITRATE OR...",0,0,53
1310 DATA "BROMIDE OR IODIDE",0,0,0,"IT'S
AN AMMONIUM COMPOUND",0,0,0
1320 DATA "END OF DATA"
```

Below is a list of changes that will enable
you to run this program on other computers
too. These instructions need to be inserted
into the program in the relevant places.

```
■ 710 LET A$=INKEY$
▲ 710 GET A$
● 705 A$=""
● 710 IF PEEK(-16384)>127 THEN GET A$
○ 710 LET A$=KEY$
● 60,350,370,490,570,600,840 HOME
▲ 60,350,370,490,570,600,840 PRINT CHR$(147)
■ 940 DIM Q$(54,38):DIM A(54,3)
```

# Formulae and equations

The chemical formula of a substance shows what elements it contains and in what proportions. In a covalent compound, it tells you the exact numbers of atoms of each element in a molecule of the substance.

## What the symbols mean

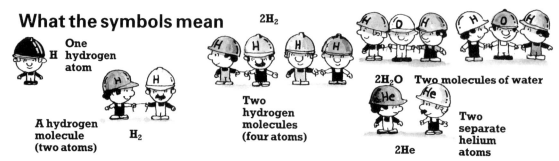

One $H$ hydrogen atom

A hydrogen molecule (two atoms) $H_2$

$2H_2$

Two hydrogen molecules (four atoms)

$2H_2O$ Two molecules of water

$2He$

Two separate helium atoms

## Balancing formulae

You may have read about how to work out formulae from valencies on page 69. Here are a few more points to remember.

Radicals, such as carbonate, have a single valency, even though they are made up of more than one element. If you have to multiply a radical, you show this in the formula by putting the number after a pair of brackets. For example, magnesium has a valency of two and nitrate has a valency of one. The formula for magnesium nitrate is $Mg(NO_3)_2$, which shows that there is one magnesium and two nitrates.

Now try working out the formula of sodium carbonate and magnesium hydroxide. Valencies: sodium (Na) 1, magnesium (Mg) 2, carbonate ($CO_3$) 2, hydroxide (OH) 1.

With an ionic compound, it is important to consider the charge on the ion, as well as its valency. An ionic compound is electrically neutral, so the charges must cancel each other out. There must be as many positives as negatives. Sodium and potassium both have valencies of one, but they cannot combine because their ions both have positive charges. However sodium will combine with chlorine which has a valency of one, because a chloride ion has a negative charge.

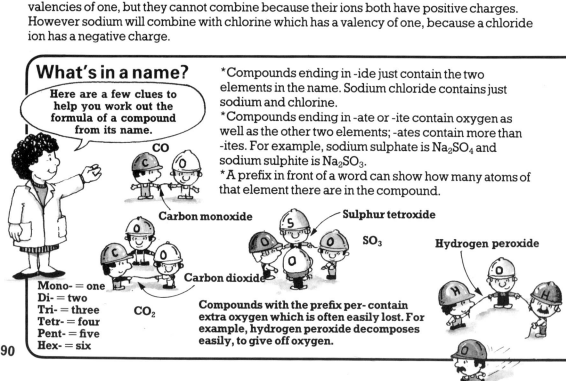

## What's in a name?

Here are a few clues to help you work out the formula of a compound from its name.

$CO$

Carbon monoxide

$CO_2$

Carbon dioxide

Mono- = one
Di- = two
Tri- = three
Tetr- = four
Pent- = five
Hex- = six

*Compounds ending in -ide just contain the two elements in the name. Sodium chloride contains just sodium and chlorine.

*Compounds ending in -ate or -ite contain oxygen as well as the other two elements; -ates contain more than -ites. For example, sodium sulphate is $Na_2SO_4$ and sodium sulphite is $Na_2SO_3$.

*A prefix in front of a word can show how many atoms of that element there are in the compound.

Sulphur tetroxide

$SO_3$

Hydrogen peroxide

Compounds with the prefix per- contain extra oxygen which is often easily lost. For example, hydrogen peroxide decomposes easily, to give off oxygen.

# Equations

Equations are a way of writing down chemical reactions in a sort of shorthand. In an equation, the formulae are used instead of the names of the chemicals. Here are some of the signs and symbols you may see in an equation.

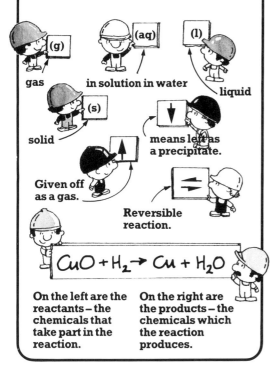

(g) gas

(aq) in solution in water

(l) liquid

(s) solid

↓ means left as a precipitate.

↑ Given off as a gas.

⇌ Reversible reaction.

$$CuO + H_2 \rightarrow Cu + H_2O$$

On the left are the reactants – the chemicals that take part in the reaction.

On the right are the products – the chemicals which the reaction produces.

# The new naming system

These days chemists are using a new system for naming compounds. It involves including the combining power of the element in the name. For example, $MnO_2$ is often called manganese dioxide, but it is also called manganese (IV) oxide. (You may have used it as a catalyst on page 72.) MnO is an ionic compound. Each oxygen ion has two negative charge, which together make four. When a manganese ion combines with two oxygen ions, it must have four positive charges, in order to cancel them out. This is why it is called manganese (IV) oxide. In other compounds, manganese can have a different valency or combining power.

# Balancing equations

A basic law of chemistry* states that you cannot create or destroy matter in a chemical reaction. Although the chemicals change their form, the same number of atoms remain. The products of a reaction may appear to be lighter than the reactants if one of the products is given off as a gas. When you write equations, you have to show that atoms are not made or destroyed. So the number of atoms on one side of an equation must be the same as on the other.

$$CuCO_3 \rightarrow CuO + CO_2$$

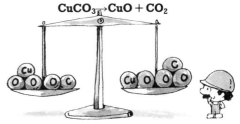

For example, look at this equation showing copper carbonate decomposing to form copper oxide and carbon dioxide. Count up the atoms and you will see that the equation balances. On each side there are three oxygens, one copper and one carbon.

Many equations are more difficult than this one. This equation for making water doesn't balance, because there is one less oxygen on the right. You can't write $H_2 + O \rightarrow H_2O$, because oxygen doesn't exist as O. The atoms always go around in pairs. Water contains twice as much hydrogen as oxygen, so try the equation with two molecules of hydrogen to one of oxygen.

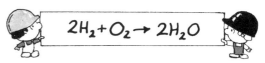

$$2H_2 + O_2 \rightarrow 2H_2O$$

If you count up the atoms, you will see that the equation is balanced. There are four hydrogens and two oxygens on each side. This shows that no atoms have been created or destroyed in the reaction.

*This is called the law of conservation of mass.

# Doing experiments

A lot of things can affect your experiments, with unexpected results. Always keep your equipment clean and dry, as dirt and traces of other chemicals can interfere with the reaction. The temperature of the room can be important too. It could be speeding up or slowing down your experiment.

With a lot of experiments, it is important to do a "control". A control is an experiment which exactly copies the experiment you are doing, except for one important factor or ingredient. For example, if you do an experiment to show the effect of a catalyst, you should also do the same experiment without the catalyst. This shows you that the catalyst is having an effect, and that the same reaction would not have happened anyway – or at least not at the same speed.

Always weigh or measure your chemicals as accurately as possible. The quantities and concentration of chemicals used can affect the reaction too. Finally, being a good scientist involves keeping detailed notes on the results of your experiments. This can help you build on what you already know, without having to do the same experiments all over again.

## Equipment and chemicals

There are a lot of experiments you can do without a proper chemistry set. You can probably find most of the equipment you need around the house, and some of the chemicals too. Here are some ideas for getting hold of chemicals and equipment you may need.

**Wooden clothes pegs make good tongs.**

**Jam jars can be used instead of test tubes. It's best to use glass containers for experiments. They are easier to see through than plastic.**

**As a funnel, you could chop off the top of a bottle of washing up liquid.**

**Droppers are useful. You can find these on old bottles of eye, ear or nose drops.**

**As filter paper, you could use coffee filters or blotting paper. (Kitchen towel doesn't work as well.)**

**Tin foil is made from aluminium. You can use this for electrodes.**

**Pencil leads can be used instead of carbon electrodes in many experiments.**

**Nichrome wire comes from electrical shops. Heat the end gently and press it into a cork. Then you can use the cork as a handle.**

**Batteries, small bulbs, thermometers and magnets will be useful for various experiments. You could use a candle to heat things, if you haven't got a spirit burner.**

**A measuring jug is useful too. You could borrow one to make your own from a jam jar. Fill the jug with water to the first measure. Pour it into your jar and make a mark on the side. You could use masking tape to write on. Then do the same for all the other measures.**

**You may be able to borrow some kitchen scales for weighing things. Use a piece of polythene or something to keep it clean.**

**You can buy rubber or plastic tubing and stoppers with holes at wine-making stores.**

**For iron, use wire wool or nails.**

**To get copper, strip the plastic from electrical wire.**

**Vinegar can be used as an acid in many experiments.**

**Crushed eggshell, marble, limestone and chalk (from chalk cliffs) are all forms of calcium carbonate.**

**You can buy a lot of chemicals at the chemist, such as iodine, sulphur and litmus papers.**

# Answers

## Page 57

A saucepan overflows when it is boiling because particles of gas take up more space than the same number of particles of liquid. As a liquid boils, it changes into a gas. When this happen, the amount of space it takes up increases.

## Page 58: Separating puzzle

To separate tea and sugar, dissolve them in cold water and then filter the solution. The tea does not dissolve, so it is filtered off. To get back the sugar, boil or evaporate the solution. You can use the same method to separate salt and flour, or a broken bottle of bath salts. To separate talc and bath salts, you could just add water. The talc does not dissolve and should float on the surface. To separate a broken jar of pins, use a magnet.

## Page 65: Atom puzzle

An atom of potassium or sodium will react with one atom or chlorine, bromine or iodine. An atom of magnesium or calcium will react with an atom of sulphur. A helium atom will not normally react at all. When larger numbers of atoms are involved, all of these atoms are able to react together, except helium.

## Page 68: Compound puzzle

Sugar, methylated spirits and bicycle oil are all covalent compounds. Epsom salts is an ionic compound.

## Page 72

Chemists keep hydrogen peroxide in dark bottles, to stop it reacting with light and decomposing.

## Page 75

Nothing can burn on the Moon because there is no oxygen there. Burning is a reaction involving oxygen.

## Page 76

Apple juice is acidic. Toothpaste and ammonia are alkaline. Paraffin and sugar are neutral. Salt is normally neutral too, but the salt we eat contains additives which make it slightly alkaline.

## Page 81

Methoxymethane is an isomer of ethanol. Its structure looks like this: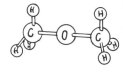

## Page 84

If sodium carbonate and zinc sulphate are dissolved together, zinc carbonate will be the precipitate.

## Page 85

The negative electrode attracts hydrogen. Water contains twice as many hydrogen atoms as oxygen atoms.

## Page 90

Sodium carbonate is $Na_2CO_3$.
Magnesium hydroxide is $Mg(OH)_2$.

# Chemistry words

**Acid.** A substance which contains hydrogen that can be replaced by a metal. In solution, it turns litmus red.

**Activation energy.** The energy needed for a reaction to occur.

**Alkali.** A substance which will neutralize an acid to produce a salt and water only. It turns litmus blue. A soluble base.

**Anion.** An ion with a negative electric charge. An atom which has gained one or more electrons.

**Anode.** A positive electrode. Electrode which discharges electrons.

**Atom.** The smallest particle of an element which can exist and still retain the properties of that element.

**Atomic number.** The number of protons in an atom of a particular element. (It equals the number of electrons.)

**Base.** The hydroxide or oxide of a metal. A substance which reacts with an acid to form a salt and water only. It does not dissolve.

**Catalyst.** A substance which alters the speed of a reaction, but remains chemically unchanged itself at the end of the reaction.

**Cathode.** A negative electrode.

**Cation.** An ion with a positive electric charge. An atom which has lost one or more electrons.

**Combustion.** Burning. Oxidation which gives out heat and light (flame).

**Compound.** A substance containing two or more elements which have been chemically combined.

**Covalent compound.** A compound made up of molecules; the molecules consist of atoms that are linked by sharing electrons.

**Decomposition.** The process of breaking down a substance into a simpler one. For example, splitting a compound into its elements.

**Electrode.** A conductor by which an electric current enters or leaves a solution during electrolysis.

**Electrolysis.** The decomposition of a substance, when melted or in solution, by passing an electric current through it.

**Electrolyte.** A substance which allows electricity to pass through it.

**Electron.** A negatively charged particle in an atom.

**Element.** A substance which cannot be split chemically into a simpler substance.

A chemical whose atoms all have the same number of protons.

**Equation.** The way chemists write down chemical reactions, using the symbols and formulae of the chemicals taking part.

**Formula.** A way of describing the composition of a substance, using symbols and numbers.

**Ion.** A charged particle; an atom or group of atoms which has lost or gained electrons.

**Ionic compound.** A compound made up of ions.

**Isotope.** Atoms of an element which have different mass numbers are different isotopes of that element.

**Lattice.** A structure in which atoms, molecules or ions are tightly bonded together in a regular pattern.

**Mass number.** The sum of protons and neutrons in the nucleus of an atom of a particular element.

**Molecule.** The smallest particle of a compound which can normally exist by itself and still have the properties of that substance.

**Neutralization.** The removal of acidity or alkalinity in a substance; the reaction between an acid and an alkali to form a salt and water.

**Neutron.** A neutral, uncharged particle in the nucleus of an atom.

**Oxidation.** The reaction between a substance and oxygen, to form an oxide. It can also mean the removal of hydrogen or the loss of electrons.

**pH scale.** The measure of acidity or alkalinity in a substance.

**Precipitate.** A solid which forms and settles in a solution.

**Products.** The substances formed as a result of a chemical change.

**Proton.** A positively charged particle in the nucleus of an atom.

**Radical.** A group of atoms or ions that form part of a molecule or larger ion and behave like a single ion.

**Reduction.** The opposite of oxidation; the removal of oxygen, the addition of hydrogen or the gain of electrons.

**Relative atomic mass.** The mass of an atom relative to the mass of an atom of carbon 12, which is said to have a mass of 12. The relative atomic mass of an element is the average mass of all the different isotopes of that element.

**Salt.** An ionic compound, formed when the hydrogen of an acid is replaced by a metal.

**Solubility.** The extent to which a substance will dissolve.

**Solution.** A soluble solid dissolved in a liquid.

**Solvent.** The medium in which a substance is dissolved.

**Suspension.** An insoluble solid suspended in a liquid; a liquid containing a substance which will not dissolve.

**Valency.** The combining power of an element; a number indicating the number of electrons gained, lost or shared in chemical bonding.

# Useful information
## Alphabetical list of elements

| | | | | | | | |
|---|---|---|---|---|---|---|---|
| Ac | Actinium | Er | Erbium | Mn | Manganese | Sm | Samarium |
| Al | Aluminium | Eu | Europium | Md | Mendelevium | Sc | Scandium |
| Am | Americium | Fm | Fermium | Hg | Mercury | Se | Selenium |
| Sb | Antimony | F | Fluorine | Mo | Molybdenum | Si | Silicon |
| Ar | Argon | Fr | Francium | Nd | Neodymium | Ag | Silver |
| As | Arsenic | Gd | Gadolinium | Ne | Neon | Na | Sodium |
| At | Astatine | Ga | Gallium | Np | Neptunium | Sr | Strontium |
| Ba | Barium | Ge | Germanium | Ni | Nickel | S | Sulphur |
| Bk | Berkelium | Au | Gold | Nb | Niobium | Ta | Tantalum |
| Be | Beryllium | Hf | Hafnium | Os | Osmium | Tc | Technetium |
| Bi | Bismuth | Ha | Hahnium | O | Oxygen | Te | Tellerium |
| B | Boron | He | Helium | Pd | Palladium | Tb | Terbium |
| Br | Bromine | Ho | Holmium | P | Phosphorus | Tl | Thallium |
| Cd | Cadmium | H | Hydrogen | Pt | Platinum | Th | Thorium |
| Cs | Caesium | In | Indium | Pu | Plutonium | Tm | Thulium |
| Ca | Calcium | I | Iodine | Po | Polonium | Sn | Tin |
| Cf | Californium | Ir | Iridium | K | Potassium | Ti | Titanium |
| C | Carbon | Fe | Iron | Pr | Praseodymium | W | Tungsten |
| Ce | Cerium | Kr | Krypton | Pm | Promethium | U | Uranium |
| Cl | Clorine | Ku | Kurtschatovium | Pa | Protoactinium | V | Vanadium |
| Cr | Chromium | La | Lanthanum | Ra | Radium | Xe | Xenon |
| Co | Cobalt | Lr | Lawrencium | Rn | Radon | Yb | Ytterbium |
| Cu | Copper | Pb | Lead | Re | Rhenium | Y | Yttrium |
| Cm | Curium | Li | Lithium | Rh | Rhodium | Zn | Zinc |
| Dy | Dysprosium | Lu | Lutetium | Rb | Rubidium | Zr | Zirconium |
| Es | Einsteinium | Mg | Magnesium | Ru | Ruthenium | | |

## Valencies of some important elements

| | | | | | |
|---|---|---|---|---|---|
| Aluminium | 3 | Copper | 1,2 | Nitrogen | 3,5 |
| Arsenic | 3,5 | Fluorine | 1 | Oxygen | 2 |
| Barium | 2 | Gold | 1 | Phosphorus | 3,5 |
| Bromine | 1 | Hydrogen | 1 | Potassium | 1 |
| Cadmium | 2 | Iodine | 1 | Rubidium | 1 |
| Caesium | 1 | Iron | 2,3 | Silicon | 4 |
| Calcium | 2 | Lead | 2,4 | Silver | 1 |
| Carbon | 4 | Lithium | 1 | Strontium | 2 |
| Chlorine | 1,7 | Magnesium | 2 | Sulphur | 2,4,6 |
| Chromium | 3,6 | Mercury | 1,2 | Tin | 2,4 |
| Cobalt | 2,3 | Nickel | 2 | Zinc | 2 |

## Activity series of metals

| | |
|---|---|
| Potassium | **most reactive** |
| Sodium | |
| Calcium | |
| Magnesium | |
| Aluminium | |
| Zinc | Copper |
| Iron | Mercury |
| Tin | Silver |
| Lead | Gold |
| Hydrogen | **least reactive** |

# Index

# INTRODUCTION TO
# BIOLOGY

**Jane Chisholm and David Beeson**

Consultant editor: Alan Alder

Designed by Iain Ashman
and Roger Priddy

Illustrated by Sue Stitt, Kuo Kang Chen, Graham Round,
Chris Shields, Ian Jackson, Aziz Khan, Chris Lyon,
David Quinn, Martin Newton and Rob McCaig.

Computer program by Christopher Smith

Program edited by Chris Oxlade

WITH
COMPUTER
PROGRAM LISTING

# Biology contents

# What is biology?

Biology is the study of all living things. It comes from two Greek words, *bios*, meaning "life", and *logos*, meaning "knowledge". Biology can be divided into lots of different branches.

Zoology is the study of animals.

Botany is the study of plants.

Ecology deals with the relationship between living things and the world around them.

Some biologists concentrate on life in a particular setting. The study of living things in the sea is called marine biology.

Others specialize in a particular kind of animal or plant. For instance, ornithologists study birds.

Over two million types, or species, of animals and plants have already been identified. Some explorers are biologists too, and new species are still being discovered.

Subjects such as medicine and agriculture are also forms of biology. The research biologists do can provide information on how to improve farming methods and breed healthier animals and crops.

The main interest of many biologists today is in studying things that are too small to be seen without a microscope. This includes learning about minute organisms, such as bacteria, and about the cells that make up animals and plants.

Biologists are also concerned about pollution and how to look after our surroundings.

99

*You can find out more about genetics on page 130.

# What do biologists do?

Biologists try to understand as much as possible about the bodies of animals and plants, and how they work. Each part of a living organism has a special job to do. It may help it move, feed or reproduce, or help it survive in a particular climate or surroundings. A biologist looks at the structures of animals and plants, and tries to work out reasons why they are the way they are. Here are a few of the questions that a biologist might ask. The answers to most of these have been found, but many others remain a mystery.

## How biology began

Many of the earliest biologists were really explorers with an interest in nature. They were usually wealthy men who went abroad and brought back specimens of animals and plants to study.

Biology did not really become organized as a science until the 18th century. Then Karl von Linne (or Linnaeus, as he is often called), a Swedish botanist, worked out a method for grouping and naming living organisms. Each animal and plant was given a name in Latin, which was the international language of scholars at that time. This system of classification* is used today by biologists all over the world.

100

**Why do the leaves of a Swiss Cheese Plant have holes in them?**

**Swiss Cheese Plants grow naturally in rocky places, which are exposed to wind. The holes may help protect the leaves from strong wind. Or they may allow light to pass through to leaves lower down the stem\*\*.**

**Why does this insect look like a stick?**

**Many animals, like this stick insect, are coloured or shaped so that they blend in with their surroundings. This is called camouflage. It prevents them from being seen and eaten by other animals.**

**Why does this flower look like an insect?**

**Many flowers need insects to help them reproduce. They have various ways of attracting the insects. The flowers of this orchid look like the female of a certain species of bee. The male bees are fooled into thinking that the flowers are female bees.**

*You can find out more about classification on page 132.
**You can find out why light is important to plants on page 106.

Why do roses and hedgehogs have thorns and prickles?

Animals and plants have prickles or stings in order to defend themselves. It's another way to avoid being eaten. Roses also use their thorns for scrambling over other plants, to reach light.

Why does the camel have a hump?

Camels live in deserts and often need to get rid of body heat quickly. Putting the fat store all in the hump allows excess heat to be lost more quickly from the rest of the body.

Why have some animals and plants died out?

**Dinosaur**

**Dodo**

**Great Auk**

Countless species, like the dinosaurs, have died out because their environments changed and they could not adapt. Many, like the great auk and the dodo, have been wiped out by human beings.

# Being a biologist

Like all scientists, a biologist has to work rather like a detective. This involves asking questions, then trying to work out the answers. A biologist works from a hunch, called a hypothesis. The hypothesis is then tested with experiments and observations.

With most biology experiments, it is important to do a "control". A control is an experiment that is the same as the experiment you are doing, except for one factor. All the other conditions must be exactly the same. This enables you to be sure whether or not the factor is influencing the result. There is advice on how to do controls with the experiments in this book.

If you're handling chemicals, remember to wash your hands after experiments. Never taste chemicals, or touch your eyes while doing an experiment.

A magnifying glass or microscope will be very useful to help you see things in more detail. You can find out about using microscopes on page 142.

Biologists often use cutaway drawings, like this one, so you can see inside an animal or plant. Many of the colours in this book are not true-to-life, but will help you see details more clearly.

You will find puzzles and questions as you read through the book. The answers to these are at the back.

# What living things have in common

Animals and plants are more alike than you might think. They all carry out certain functions which are common to all living things. One of the jobs of a biologist is to find out how each animal and plant is adapted to carry out these functions. From page 106 onwards, you can find out about them in more detail.

## 1 Food

All living things need food, just as cars need fuel. Food gives them energy for the activities going on inside their bodies. Plants make their own food from sunlight, water and a gas in the air called carbon dioxide. Animals get their food by eating plants or other animals.

Sun

Carbon dioxide

## 2 Respiration

In order to get energy from food, animals and plants carry out a process called respiration. In most cases, this involves taking in oxygen and giving out carbon dioxide. Plants exchange these gases through tiny holes in their leaves. Animals can take in oxygen in a variety of ways. For instance, fish can absorb oxygen from water through their gills.

## 3 Waste

Respiration and feeding also produce waste substances which the animal or plant does not need. Getting rid of them is called excretion. Plants excrete through their leaves. Humans do it in various ways, such as sweating, breathing out and going to the toilet.

### Breathing test

You can do a test to show that you breathe out carbon dioxide. Put some limewater* in a jar. Limewater is a clear liquid which goes milky if you mix it with carbon dioxide. Blow into the jar with a straw. What happens?

Use sprouting seeds, such as mung beans (bean shoots).

Keep the lid on during the experiment.

Put them in a piece of loose-woven material, such as gauze or muslin.

Limewater

You can do a similar test with plants, though it may take a few days before you get a reaction.

## 4 Sensitivity

Have you ever noticed that crocuses only open their petals when the sun is shining? All living things are sensitive to changes in their surroundings, though some are more sensitive than others. Mammals have a wide range of senses. For instance, a zebra can use its sight, hearing and smell to sense a lion approaching.

*You can buy this at the chemist's.

## 5 Movement

All living things move, even though plants usually move too slowly for you to see. If you leave a potted plant by a window for a few days, you may find that the leaves have turned towards the window. Most animals can move their whole bodies, whereas plants can only move parts of them. Moving your whole body, so that you can get from place to place, is called locomotion.

## 6 Growth

All living things grow. Some organisms, such as trees, keep on growing throughout their lives. Others, like us, reach a certain size and then stop. Some organisms, such as plants, do most of their growing at certain times of year.

## 7 Reproduction

Nothing lives forever, so it is important that all living things should be able to produce offspring, or new versions of themselves. This is called reproduction.

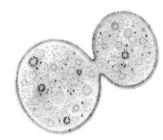

Microscopic organisms, such as the one shown above, can reproduce simply by dividing in two. This is called asexual reproduction, which means that the new organism is produced from only one parent.

Most animals and plants reproduce sexually, from two parents. A new animal or plant is produced when a male sex cell joins a female sex cell, in a process called fertilization. The male sex cells in flowering plants are contained in a powder called pollen. Insects often help carry pollen to the female sex cells of other plants.

### Why isn't a car a living thing?

In many ways a car is just like a living thing. It needs food (petrol) and it excretes waste (from the exhaust pipe). It turns the food into energy in the combustion chambers. It moves and it is sensitive to the touch of the hand on the steering wheel. So why isn't it alive?

# What are living things made of?

All living organisms are made up of tiny things called cells, each containing lots of different parts. Your body has about 50 billion cells; some microscopic organisms only have one. Cells were first discovered in the 17th century, by an English scientist, Robert Hooke. Most cells can only be seen with a very powerful microscope*, but you can see some with an ordinary one. There are many kinds of cells, but they all have the same basic features. Try to imagine a cell as a sort of factory. Each part has a special job to do.

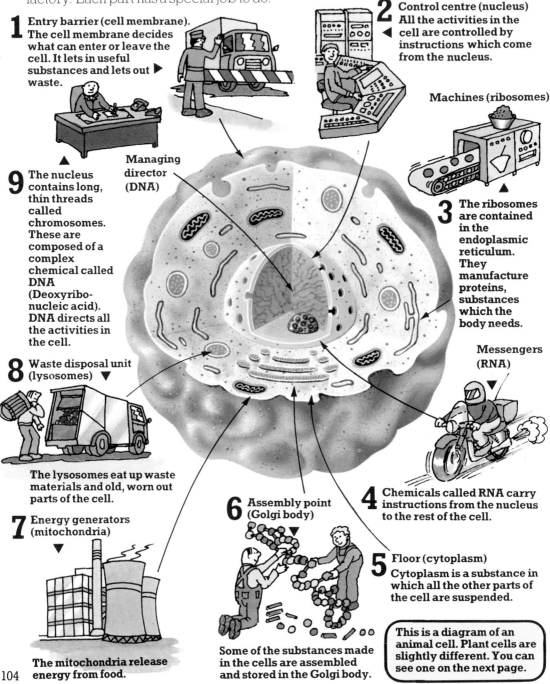

**1** Entry barrier (cell membrane). The cell membrane decides what can enter or leave the cell. It lets in useful substances and lets out ▶ waste.

**2** Control centre (nucleus) All the activities in the cell are controlled by instructions which come from the nucleus.

Machines (ribosomes)

Managing director (DNA)

**9** The nucleus contains long, thin threads called chromosomes. These are composed of a complex chemical called DNA (Deoxyribonucleic acid). DNA directs all the activities in the cell.

**3** The ribosomes are contained in the endoplasmic reticulum. They manufacture proteins, substances which the body needs.

Messengers (RNA)

**8** Waste disposal unit (lysosomes) ▼

The lysosomes eat up waste materials and old, worn out parts of the cell.

**7** Energy generators (mitochondria) ▼

**6** Assembly point (Golgi body) ▼

**4** Chemicals called RNA carry instructions from the nucleus to the rest of the cell.

**5** Floor (cytoplasm) Cytoplasm is a substance in which all the other parts of the cell are suspended.

The mitochondria release energy from food.

Some of the substances made in the cells are assembled and stored in the Golgi body.

This is a diagram of an animal cell. Plant cells are slightly different. You can see one on the next page.

104

*See page 142 to find out about looking at cells with a microscope.

# Plant cells

Plant cells are larger than animal cells, and are often oblong in shape. They have a few extra features that animal cells do not have. Here is a diagram of a plant cell.

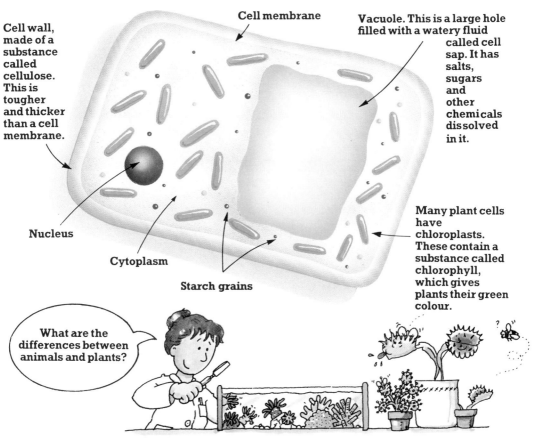

Cell membrane

Cell wall, made of a substance called cellulose. This is tougher and thicker than a cell membrane.

Vacuole. This is a large hole filled with a watery fluid called cell sap. It has salts, sugars and other chemicals dissolved in it.

Nucleus

Cytoplasm

Starch grains

Many plant cells have chloroplasts. These contain a substance called chlorophyll, which gives plants their green colour.

What are the differences between animals and plants?

The differences between animals and plants are not always as obvious as it might seem. There are plants that eat animals, and animals, such as corals and sea anemones, that look rather like plants. In the case of some microscopic organisms, biologists often disagree about which category they belong to. Here is a general guide to the differences between them.

## Differences between animals and plants

\*Animals take in food, by means of a mouth, or similar organ. Plants make their own food from sunlight, carbon dioxide and water.

\*Most animals are capable of locomotion; most plants are not.

\*Animals are more sensitive than plants. Plants only respond slowly to changes around them.

\*Most plants contain chlorophyll and cellulose. No animal contains these.

## Animal and plant puzzles

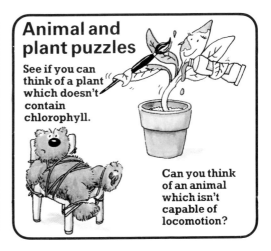

See if you can think of a plant which doesn't contain chlorophyll.

Can you think of an animal which isn't capable of locomotion?

# Making food

All living organisms need food, to provide energy for the cells to carry out their activities, and for growth and repair. Plants are able to make food, by capturing some of the Sun's energy. They do this in a process called photosynthesis, which means "making things with light". Plants are the only organisms capable of doing this. All animals depend on them – directly or indirectly – for their food.

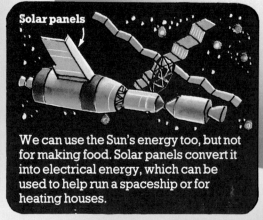

**Solar panels**

We can use the Sun's energy too, but not for making food. Solar panels convert it into electrical energy, which can be used to help run a spaceship or for heating houses.

## How plants make food

To make food, plants need sunlight, chlorophyll, carbon dioxide and water. The leaves are a plant's main food factories. The chlorophyll contained in many of their cells is used to trap sunlight.

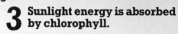

**Carbon dioxide**     **Sunlight**

**1** Carbon dioxide from the air enters the leaves through tiny pores called stomata.

**2** Water from the soil rises up through very thin tubes in the stem and then travels through a network of tiny veins. You can see these veins if you look very closely at a leaf.

**3** Sunlight energy is absorbed by chlorophyll.

**4** A chemical reaction using the trapped energy takes place in the chloroplasts (the chlorophyll-containing cells). They make glucose (a kind of sugar) from the water and carbon dioxide. In many plants this is then converted to starch.

Chlorophyll making glucose

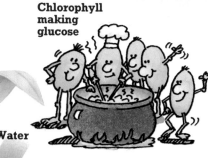

**Water**

Leaf cell, magnified even more.

Cross-section of a leaf, magnified to about 30 times its real size.

Stomata

Leaves are usually thin and flat, so that as much chlorophyll as possible is exposed to the light.

Plants make other kinds of food too. To do this they need minerals, such as nitrates and phosphates, which are found in the soil. These are dissolved in water and absorbed through a plant's roots.

106

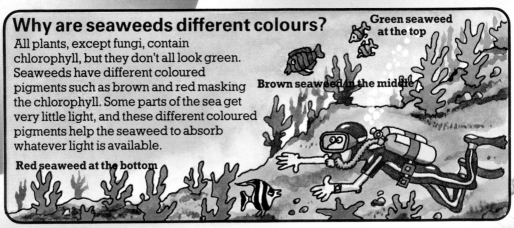

## Why are seaweeds different colours?

All plants, except fungi, contain chlorophyll, but they don't all look green. Seaweeds have different coloured pigments such as brown and red masking the chlorophyll. Some parts of the sea get very little light, and these different coloured pigments help the seaweed to absorb whatever light is available.

Green seaweed at the top

Brown seaweed in the middle

Red seaweed at the bottom

## Starch experiment

This experiment proves that plants need light and chlorophyll to make starch. Use a variegated plant (e.g. geranium) with green and non-green leaf parts.

**1** Put the plant in a dark cupboard for a couple of days to stop it carrying out photosynthesis. This uses up its starch.

**2** Pour methylated spirits into a glass jar to a depth of about 3cm. DO NOT use a lid. Then fill a small saucepan with water to a depth of about 4cm. Bring it to the boil, turn off the heat and put the saucepan on a cool ring.

Using oven gloves, carefully lower the jar into the water. Drop a leaf from the plant into the water, beside the jar. After a few seconds, use cooking tongs to pick up the leaf and drop it into the methylated spirits. This will remove the colour after a few minutes.

**Cut-away picture**

**Glass jar**

**Methylated spirits**

**Cold ring** **Cooking tongs**

Be careful! Keep methylated spirits away from the hot cooker ring.

**3** Wash the leaf and add a few drops of iodine solution\*. If the leaf goes blue-black, it contains starch, so you need to leave the plant a bit longer. If it goes brown, there is no starch left.

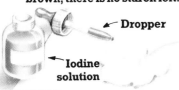

**Dropper**

**Iodine solution**

**4** Attach a piece of black paper to both sides of a leaf on the plant. Leave it in a sunny place for a day. Draw a diagram of the leaf.

**Paper clip** **Black paper**

**5** After a day, remove the leaf and test for starch. The results should correspond with your diagram. Only the green parts which were left uncovered should contain starch.

**Diagram of leaf**

**Result of starch test**

Not all plants make starch from glucose. You could try this experiment on a variety of plants to find out which ones do.

*You can buy this at a chemist's.

# Feeding

As animals cannot make their own food, they get theirs by eating plants, or animals that have eaten plants. In doing so, energy passes from the plant to the animal that eats it, and so on. Biologists call this an energy flow, or a food chain. Here you can see an example of a food chain. With each link in the chain, the amount of energy transferred gets smaller. This is because some of it has already been used up by the animal or plant in carrying out its activities.

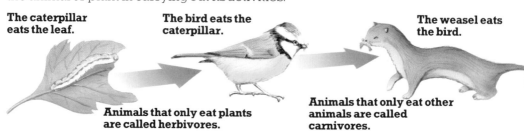

**The caterpillar eats the leaf.**

**The bird eats the caterpillar.**

**The weasel eats the bird.**

**Animals that only eat plants are called herbivores.**

**Animals that only eat other animals are called carnivores.**

Food chains are often more complicated than this, because many animals eat a variety of things. When a food chain has several different branches, biologists call it a food web.

**Animals, like us, that eat plants and animals are called omnivores.**

## Herbivores and carnivores

Herbivores and carnivores have features to suit their different eating habits. Carnivores need good long-distance eyesight, in order to spot their prey, and they have to be able to move quickly and quietly to catch it. Herbivores need to be able to see animals approaching from all directions, so that they can avoid being eaten. For instance, look at the differences between a cat and a mouse.

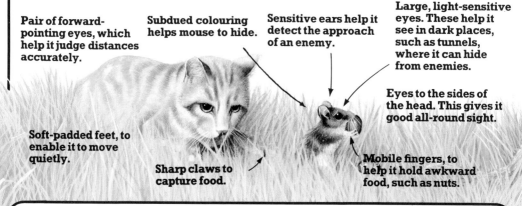

**Pair of forward-pointing eyes, which help it judge distances accurately.**

**Subdued colouring helps mouse to hide.**

**Sensitive ears help it detect the approach of an enemy.**

**Large, light-sensitive eyes. These help it see in dark places, such as tunnels, where it can hide from enemies.**

**Eyes to the sides of the head. This gives it good all-round sight.**

**Soft-padded feet, to enable it to move quietly.**

**Sharp claws to capture food.**

**Mobile fingers, to help it hold awkward food, such as nuts.**

## Eyesight test

Animals with eyes to the sides of their heads can't judge distances very accurately. This is because the pictures they form with each eye don't overlap very much. Animals like us, with eyes at the front of their heads, have binocular vision. This means that they use both eyes together. Try holding a pencil almost at arm's length. Then, with one eye closed, try to touch the top very quickly with one of your fingers. Then try it with both eyes. Which is more accurate?

# How food is recycled

When animals and plants die, their bodies rot and eventually disappear into the soil. Rotting is caused by organisms, such as bacteria or fungi, which are known as decomposers. Decomposers feed on the dead bodies of animals and plants. They break them down into simple raw materials and release nitrates and other substances into the soil. These are absorbed by plants and used to help them make food.

**Plants**

The blue arrows show energy used up by the animal or plant for its own activities.

**Carnivores**

**Decomposers**

**Herbivores**

**Carnivores**

The orange arrows show energy passed along the food chain.

The purple arrows show all parts of the food chain returning to the soil, to be used again by plants.

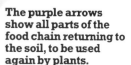

# Mouths

Animals feed in a variety of different ways. Their mouths are adapted for the kind of food they eat.

Butterflies and moths feed on nectar in flowers. They have a long, coiled tube called a proboscis, which uncoils to reach inside the flower. ▼

◀ Insect-eating birds often have long, pointed beaks, to help them look for food inside cracks in trees.

Seed-eating birds tend to have short, blunt beaks to pick up the seeds. ◀

Snails eat grass, leaves and flowers. A snail has a rough-edged tongue, rather like a file, which can scrape off bits of vegetation. ▼

# Monkey puzzle

Why do you think animals that live in trees have forward-pointing eyes?

# Carnivorous plants

Some plants live in soils which are poor in nitrates. They can make up for this by catching insects and other animals that contain the chemicals they need. The Venus Fly-Trap catches flies, dissolves them and absorbs the liquid.

109

# What happens to food

Food contains many different, useful substances, such as proteins, carbohydrates and fats. But in order for the body to make use of them, the food has to get inside the cells. The food you eat wouldn't fit into tiny cells, so it has to go through several processes first. It is chewed with the teeth, and then digested, or broken down, into smaller, simpler chemicals. These chemicals dissolve in the blood, which carries them round the body to the cells.

## Teeth

Mammals' teeth come in different shapes and sizes, to suit their different eating habits.

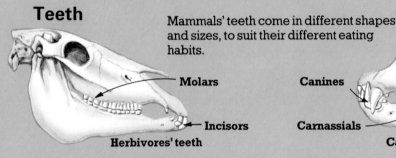

Molars

Canines

Incisors

Carnassials

**Herbivores' teeth**

**Carnivores' teeth**

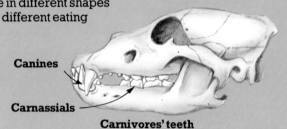

Plants contain a lot of fibrous material that is difficult to digest, so herbivores have to chew their food a lot before swallowing it. Herbivores have flat, ridged teeth, called molars, to grind their food and sharp front teeth, called incisors, to cut it. Carnivores have long, pointed teeth, called canines, for

seizing their prey. Their back teeth, or carnassials, are for slicing meat into small pieces. Humans have canines, molars and incisors too, but the differences between them are not as pronounced as in other animals. This is because we eat a lot of different things.

## Jaws

The jaws of herbivores and carnivores vary too. Dogs move their jaws up and down to slice their food. Horses and cows move their jaws round and round in a circular grinding motion.

## What food is used for

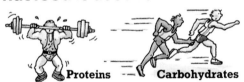

Proteins

Carbohydrates

Fats

**Vitamins and minerals**

*Proteins give you energy and build you up. They enable you to grow, and to replace dead cells as they wear away. The main protein foods are meat, fish, eggs, milk and vegetables like lentils.
*Carbohydrates are the main energy-giving foods. You find carbohydrates in starchy foods, such as bread, potatoes, yams, rice and pasta, and in sugary foods, such as sweets and cakes.

*Fats give energy too, and can provide a store of food beneath your skin and help keep you warm. Fats are found in milk, butter, cream, cheese and meat.
*Many foods also contain vitamins and minerals. You only need small quantities of these, but they are very important for keeping different parts of the body in good condition.

# Digestion

Once you've swallowed your food, it begins a long journey which ends in the cells. Digestion starts in the mouth and continues in the gut, or alimentary canal. This is a tube about 7m long, which stretches from the mouth to the anus. Food is broken down by digestive juices, which contain important chemicals called enzymes. All animals have some kind of digestive system. Here you can find out about the human digestive system.

## What do enzymes do?

Enzymes help speed up digestion. Without them the process would take much longer. Carbohydrates are broken down into sugars, such as glucose. Proteins are broken down into amino acids. Fats are broken down into glycerol and fatty acids.

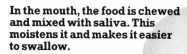

Enzymes

## Saliva experiment

Saliva contains an enzyme which digests starch. Try chewing a piece of bread for a few minutes without swallowing it. It will start to taste sweet, which shows that the starch has been turned into a sugar.

## Jelly and pineapple experiment

Pineapple contains an enzyme which digests protein. You could try this experiment to show how it does this. Jelly contains a protein called gelatine. Make two small jellies, one with fresh pineapple and one with tinned pineapple. The one with fresh pineapple won't set properly, because the enzyme breaks down the gelatine. Enzymes only work at certain temperatures. Tinned pineapple has been boiled first, which destroys the enzyme. So the jelly with tinned pineapple should set properly.

In the mouth, the food is chewed and mixed with saliva. This moistens it and makes it easier to swallow.

As you swallow, your tongue pushes food into your throat and down the oesophagus.

Mouth

Food is squeezed along the gut by two layers of muscles contracting alternately. This is called peristalsis.

The stomach stores food and controls its flow to the rest of the gut. It releases digestive juices and an acid, which helps kill any bacteria.

Oesophagus

One of the liver's jobs is to make a green liquid called bile, which helps break up fats.

Liver

Stomach

Pancreas

Large intestine

Digestive juices are released into the duodenum from the pancreas. These contain enzymes which can digest all types of food.

Duodenum

Ileum

Digestion is completed in the ileum. The wall of the ileum contains lots of finger-like structures called villi. The walls of the villi are only one cell thick. Digested food can pass through them and into tiny blood vessels on the other side.

Anus

Some of the things you eat, known as roughage, cannot be digested. They pass along the large intestine to the anus, where they are eliminated from the body.

# Getting energy

Food alone cannot provide energy for living organisms to use. The energy has to be released from the food in a chemical reaction called respiration. Food is rather like a fuel, such as coal. Coal is a source of energy which can be used to drive machinery and keep us warm. But it can't do this on its own. Before it can give off energy, it has to be combined with oxygen from the air and burned. It is the same with food. In order to release energy from food, most organisms have to combine it with oxygen. They give off carbon dioxide as a waste product. This is why you need to breathe.

## How the energy is used

Your body uses energy in various ways. It powers your muscles, so you can move. It helps you grow and gives your cells energy, so they can carry out their activities. Some energy is released as heat, which keeps your body warm. In some animals, it is released as light or electricity.

**Firefly**

**Glow-worm**

**Electric eel**

## Keeping the gases circulating

Green plants help to keep the gases in the air balanced. They take in oxygen and give out carbon dioxide just as animals do. But during photosynthesis, they take in even larger quantities of carbon dioxide and give out large amounts of oxygen as waste. Without plants, the supply of oxygen in the air would eventually run out.

**Oxygen**

**Carbon dioxide**

*See page 106.*

## How living things respire

In order to carry out respiration, most animals and plants need to take in oxygen and give out carbon dioxide. Biologists call this "exchanging gases". Plants do it through the stomata* in their leaves. Many animals exchange gases by breathing. Oxygen is taken in through the nose or mouth and into the windpipe and lungs, where it passes into the bloodstream. Here a pair of lungs has been cut away so you can see inside.

**Bronchi (pronounced brong-kee)**

**Bronchioles**

The windpipe divides into two main passages called bronchi. These split up into hundreds of tiny tubes, called bronchioles, rather like the branches of a tree.

Why do you pant after exercise?

## What is aerobics?

Respiration which uses oxygen is called "aerobic" respiration. Aerobics is the name given to exercise which increases the flow of oxygen around the body. It is hard, but not exhausting, and can be kept up for a long time. Exercise such as sprinting is "anaerobic", because you have to produce a lot of energy too fast for your body to cope aerobically. You can respire anaerobically for a short time. Too much anaerobic respiration produces lactic acid in your muscles, which makes them ache and gives you cramp.

# What happens when you breathe?

When you breathe in, tiny air sacs, called alveoli, fill with air. Oxygen in the air passes through the walls of the alveoli into tiny blood vessels. The blood carries the oxygen to the cells, where it is exchanged for waste carbon dioxide. Carbon dioxide is carried back to the lungs and breathed out.

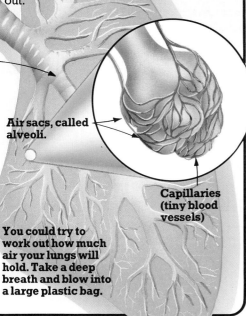

**Air sacs, called alveoli.**

**Capillaries (tiny blood vessels)**

**You could try to work out how much air your lungs will hold. Take a deep breath and blow into a large plastic bag.**

# Energy experiment

You could try this experiment to show that plants, as well as animals, give off energy in respiration. You can test this by finding out whether they produce heat. Use sprouting seeds, such as mung beans (bean sprouts)*.

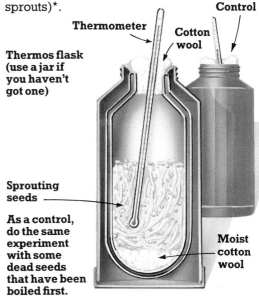

**Control**

**Thermometer**

**Cotton wool**

**Thermos flask (use a jar if you haven't got one)**

**Sprouting seeds**

**As a control, do the same experiment with some dead seeds that have been boiled first.**

**Moist cotton wool**

After a few days, read the two thermometers. You should find that the temperature of the one containing the live seeds is higher than the other one.

# How other animals exchange gases

All gas exchange systems have certain things in common. They need to be moist and in close contact with the air and blood (or other circulation system), so that oxygen can get to the cells.

Birds have a very efficient breathing system, with lungs that extend even into some bones. Birds appear to breathe as they beat their wings – about 200 times a minute.

Birds that are powerful fliers need to be able to take in plenty of air. The intake of air is helped by the movement of their limbs. For example, when a heron walks, its leg action draws enough air in and out. When it flies, the greater wing muscle activity draws much more air in and out.

 An insect's gas exchange system consists of a series of tubes running through its body, with tiny pores opening on to the outside.

Fish absorb oxygen from water through their gills, which contain tiny capillaries.

 Frogs can breathe in several ways, including through their moist skin.

## Anaerobes

Some organisms, known as anaerobes, can respire anaerobically all the time. They often live deep in the soil, where there is little oxygen. Yeast is partly an anaerobe. Wine is made by yeast carrying out anaerobic respiration. The yeast feeds on grape juice and gives off carbon dioxide, without using oxygen.

*You can get these from a health food or garden shop.

# How substances move around the body

All living things need some method of moving substances around their bodies. Food and oxygen have to be taken to the cells, and waste, such as carbon dioxide, has to be taken away from them. In plants, food and water are carried by bundles of tubes called the phloem and xylem. In animals, food and other substances are carried by the blood. Biologists refer to these as transport systems.

## What does blood do?

Blood does a number of different jobs. It carries substances to and from the cells, it eats up germs and helps repair wounds by clotting. Blood is made up of a liquid called plasma, which contains blood cells and dissolved particles of food and waste. There are three main types of blood cells.

**Red blood cells carry the oxygen. They contain a red pigment, or colouring, called haemoglobin. Red blood cells wear out and are replaced about every four months.**

**White blood cells are larger, but not nearly as numerous as red ones. Their main job is to eat up bacteria and fight infections. They only last a few days.**

**Platelets are tiny fragments of cells, which help the blood to clot when you cut yourself.**

## What is a heartbeat?

A heartbeat is the sound made by the heart valves closing. The heart usually beats about 70 times a minute. You can hear it if you put your ear to someone's chest. You can get an even louder sound if you use a microphone and put the sound through an amplifier onto a tape.

## How blood gets around the body

Blood circulates the body in tubes, called blood vessels. This process is kept going by the heart, which is a pump made of muscle. There are three types of blood vessels. Vessels which carry blood to the heart are called veins. They have valves to

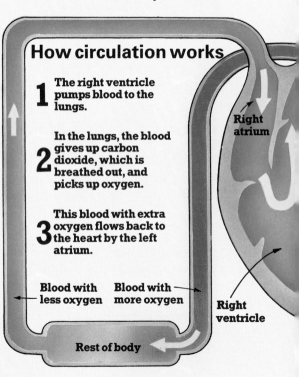

### How circulation works

**1** The right ventricle pumps blood to the lungs.

**2** In the lungs, the blood gives up carbon dioxide, which is breathed out, and picks up oxygen.

**3** This blood with extra oxygen flows back to the heart by the left atrium.

Blood with less oxygen

Blood with more oxygen

Right atrium

Right ventricle

Rest of body

## Test your pulse

Every time your heart beats, there is a rush of blood along the arteries, away from the heart. You can feel this as a sort of throb, called a pulse, on your wrist. Press lightly with one or two fingers on the largest artery. It is not always easy to find the right place, so you may have to try several times. Time it to see how many beats there are in a minute. Try again after exercise, such as running. How much difference is there?

## Did you know?

You have so many capillaries in your body that they would stretch round the world twice, if you laid them end to end.

ensure that the blood flows in the right direction. Vessels which carry blood away from the heart are called arteries. Capillaries are narrow, thin-walled vessels, through which substances such as food and oxygen can pass into the blood.

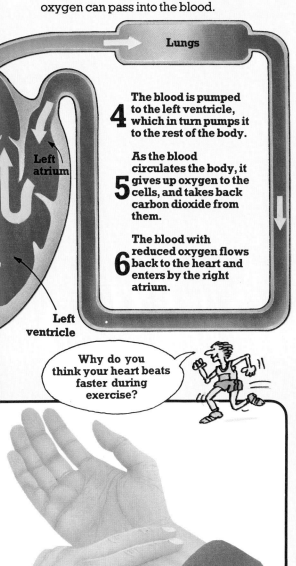

Lungs

**4** The blood is pumped to the left ventricle, which in turn pumps it to the rest of the body.

**5** As the blood circulates the body, it gives up oxygen to the cells, and takes back carbon dioxide from them.

**6** The blood with reduced oxygen flows back to the heart and enters by the right atrium.

Left atrium

Left ventricle

Why do you think your heart beats faster during exercise?

## How do substances get in and out of cells?

Carbon dioxide diffusing out

Oxygen diffusing in

The cell membrane decides which substances may enter or leave a cell. There are several methods by which it does this, not all of which are fully understood by biologists. Many simple substances, such as oxygen, pass through by a method known as diffusion.

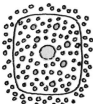

Particles diffusing across cell membrane

Equal concentration of particles

Diffusion happens when there are more particles of certain substances in one area than in another. Some of those particles then move across, so that there is an equal concentration of them everywhere. The diffusion of water is known as osmosis.

## Potato chip experiment

You could watch osmosis at work with uncooked potato chips. Put some in a bowl of very salty water. As a control, leave some others in a bowl of ordinary water. After about an hour, the ones in salty water should be limp. Potato cells contain a lot of water. The solution of salt water is more concentrated than the solution inside the cells. So water passes into it from the potato cells, making the potatoes limp. This is why you shouldn't put too much plant food in the water when you're watering your plants.

# Plant transport systems

The transport system in plants consists of bundles of tubes in the stem, branches and roots. These tubes are called the phloem (pronounced flo-em) and xylem (pronounced zy-lem). The phloem vessels carry the food manufactured in the leaves to all parts of the plant. The xylem vessels carry water and dissolved minerals from the roots to the rest of the plant.

Water is constantly travelling through a plant. It is taken in through the roots by osmosis and evaporates from the leaves in a process called transpiration. Transpiration cools the leaves and protects them from the Sun. It also causes a kind of suction, which pulls water up the stem from the roots.

Water evaporates from the leaves into the air.

Water sucked up the stem or trunk.

## Controlling water loss

Plants lose more water from their leaves when it's hot or very windy. They lose less when it's still or humid. To keep healthy, plants need to maintain a steady water content. So many plants are adapted to prevent them losing too much water.

Why do you think cacti have spines as leaves?

Why do you think trees lose their leaves in winter?

## Phloem and xylem

Here you can see a slice through the stem, showing the phloem and xylem vessels.

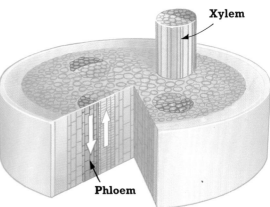

Xylem

Phloem

## Plants and water

You could try this experiment to show water being sucked up a stem. Mix a teaspoonful of food colouring with a mugful of water and put it into a jar with a cut plant. Choose one with a transparent stem, such as celery. Leave the plant for a few hours.

Water has been sucked up to here.

You will be able to see from the dye how far the water has travelled up the stem. If the plant doesn't have a transparent stem, cut slices off so you can see inside.

Another way to show that water is taken up by the plant is to mark the water level on the jar when you begin. Cover the water with oil, to stop it evaporating.

Coloured dye and water

## Which side of a leaf loses most water?

To find the answer, tape dry cobalt chloride paper* to both sides of a leaf. As it comes in contact with water, the paper will turn from blue to pink. Which side goes pink first?

Cobalt chloride paper

Water absorbed by the roots.

*You can buy cobalt chloride paper at most chemists.

# Waste disposal

All animals need to keep the substances inside their bodies at a safe level. This is called homeostasis. This involves regulating the supply of substances, such as glucose and oxygen, in the blood, and getting rid of waste, or excretion. In mammals this is carried out by the lungs (which excrete carbon dioxide), the skin (which removes excess heat), the liver and kidneys. These are called the excretory organs.

## What the liver does

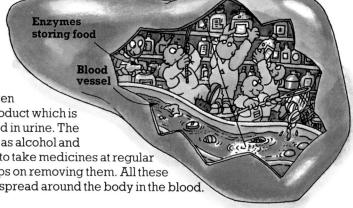

Enzymes storing food

Blood vessel

The liver contains hundreds of enzymes*, which help it do a variety of jobs. Any food not immediately needed by the cells is taken to the liver and stored. Excess proteins are broken down to release urea, a waste product which is taken to the kidneys and excreted in urine. The liver also removes poisons, such as alcohol and medicines. This is why you have to take medicines at regular intervals – because the liver keeps on removing them. All these activities produce heat, which is spread around the body in the blood.

## Liver enzyme experiment

You could try this experiment to see a liver enzyme at work. Many cells produce a waste product called hydrogen peroxide. Liver contains an enzyme called catalase, which breaks this down into water and oxygen.

**Dilute two teaspoonsful of hydrogen peroxide** in a mugful of water and put it in a jar with a piece of uncooked liver.**

**If catalase is present, you should see bubbles of oxygen gas given off. The control may give off bubbles, too, but much fewer.**

Control

**Be careful! Keep hydrogen peroxide away from your skin and eyes.**

Bubbles of gas

Liver

Hydrogen peroxide

**As a control, put some diluted hydrogen peroxide in a jar without liver.**

**Other animals and plants contain catalase. You could try the same experiment with celery or potato.**

## What the kidneys do

The kidneys are the main excretory organs. Each one contains over a million microscopic filtering units, called nephrons. The kidneys filter the blood, removing urea, excess salts and water. Together these form a liquid called urine, which travels along two tubes, called ureters, to the bladder. The bladder empties when you go to the toilet. The kidneys control the amount of water in your body. The more you drink, the more urine you produce.

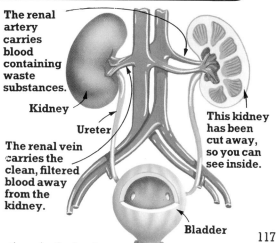

The renal artery carries blood containing waste substances.

Kidney

Ureter

The renal vein carries the clean, filtered blood away from the kidney.

This kidney has been cut away, so you can see inside.

Bladder

*Enzymes are chemicals which speed up reactions in the body.
**You can buy hydrogen peroxide at the chemist's.

117

# Skeletons and movement

All animals and plants need some means of supporting their bodies. Otherwise they would lose shape and collapse. A skeleton is one kind of support. It provides an animal with a rigid frame, which gives it shape and enables it to move. All animals need to be able to move – to find food, or a mate, or to defend themselves from attack. Plants move too, though their movements are more limited*.

**Jellyfish**     **Seaweed**

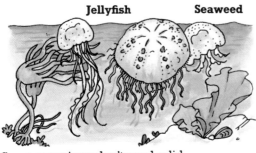

Many plants are supported by the pressure of water in their cells, and will flop over if they don't get enough water. (But trees are supported by the wood in their stems.) A few animals, such as caterpillars, are supported by the pressure of water in their bodies.

Some organisms don't need solid skeletons. Sea creatures, such as jellyfish and seaweed are supported by fluid inside their bodies, and by the water itself. Seaweed is much too limp to stand up by itself on land.

You can support yourself quite easily in water too. Try supporting the weight of your whole body on a couple of fingers.

## External skeletons

**Beetle**

Some animals, such as insects and crabs, have an external skeleton, called an exoskeleton. It is rather like a suit of armour, made up of hard plates and tubes with moveable joints.

## Moving in the air

To fly, an animal needs to be light, to have something to push against the air, and a shape which will keep it there.

Birds have very light, hollow bones and powerful muscles attached to their wings.

### How lift works

The shape of a bird's wing forces air to move more quickly across the top of it than underneath it. Hold a small strip of paper (about 2cm by 7cm) by one end so that it hangs in a roughly horizontal curve, away from you. Blow gently along the top of it. You'll see it rise as the moving air generates lift.

Birds' wings are light and have a large surface area. Their shape provides a force called a lift, which helps the bird stay in the air.

These are called contour feathers. They work like tiles, covering the base of the wing, giving it a smooth, streamlined shape.

These are called flight feathers. They are hollow and light and are held together by hundreds of tiny hooks.

*You can find out about plant movement on page 120.

# Internal skeletons

Mammals, birds, fish, reptiles and amphibians all have an internal skeleton made up of bones and cartilage, or gristle.

Bones are held together at joints, by fibres called ligaments. The joints are kept well oiled by a lubricating fluid, called synovial fluid. There are several kinds of joints.

**The neck contains a pivot joint. This allows you to swivel your head from side to side.**

## Did you know?

A giraffe has the same number of bones in its neck as a human.

**Knees, elbows and fingers are hinge joints. They move backwards and forwards like a door.**

**The hip is a ball and socket joint. It enables you to move your leg in practically any direction.**

# What are bones made of?

Bones are strong yet flexible, because of the calcium and protein they contain. Boiling them in water for a long time removes the protein, so the next time you or someone in your family makes some meat stock, you can see the effect. The protein in the liquid sets like jelly when it cools, while the bones become white and brittle. To remove calcium, leave another bone in dilute hydrochloric acid* for a few days. This makes it bendy and rubbery.

# Moving in water

Water is much denser, or heavier, than air. This is why walking in water is slower than walking on land. Fish, however, are specially adapted for moving in water. The fastest fish can move almost as fast as a cheetah.

**A fish has a swim-bladder filled with gases, which helps it to rise and sink in the water.**

**A fish swims by sweeping its body from side to side. It has powerful muscles on each side of its backbone.**

**The fins act rather like rudders on a boat.**

**A fish's body has a streamlined shape.**

# Muscles

Muscles are attached to the joints by strong, non-stretchy fibres called tendons. They pull against the skeleton and enable it to move. Muscles can pull bones towards them, by contracting, but they cannot push.

*Ask for "normal" hydrochloric acid at the chemist.

# Sensitivity

Sensitivity is essential for survival. All animals and plants are capable of sensing changes in their environment. A change in light, sound, smell, touch or temperature, is known as a stimulus. Most animals have sense organs, such as ears or eyes, which are adapted to receive a particular stimulus. The organs contain sensitive cells, which receive information and pass it to the brain by means of nerves*. Animals are not all sensitive to the same things. Some have a wide range of senses; others rely almost entirely on one sense. Plants don't have distinct sense organs, but certain parts of their bodies are sensitive to particular stimuli.

## Light and vision

Most organisms are sensitive to light, but not all are capable of vision. Vision means using eyes to form a picture of the world around you. The eyes take in light rays, which are focussed by a lens on to light-sensitive cells at the back of the eye. The cells send messages to the brain, which interprets them as what you see.

**Insects have compound eyes, made up of large numbers of tiny lenses. The picture they see is probably rather blurred. Dragonflies rely almost entirely on sight. They have nearly 30,000 lenses in each eye.** Dragonfly's eyes

**Bees can see ultra-violet light, which we cannot see. This enables them to see lines on the petals of flowers, which guides them towards nectar.**

**Animals that live by night, such as owls, often have big eyes. This helps them take in as much light as is available.**

What we see

What the bee sees

### Plants and light

Plants respond to light by growing towards or away from it. (Some prefer shade.) This experiment shows you which part of a plant is sensitive to light.
**Grow some cabbage, tomato or cereal seeds in seed compost.**
**When they are about 10mm high, cover the tips of half of them with silver foil. Leave about 7mm of stem exposed.**

Silver foil

**Put the box next to a window or a bright lamp.**

After a few days, the uncovered shoots should have started to bend and grow towards the light. The covered ones should still be straight, showing that it is the tip of the shoot that detects light. The plant does most of its growing just beneath the tip.

## How flowers respond to light

Some flowers, such as crocuses, only open their petals on sunny days. Others open and close at certain times of day. Some gardeners make flower clocks. The flowers are arranged in a circle, according to the time of day they open or close.

These are called evening primroses, because they don't open until about 6 p.m.

120

*You can find out more about nerves on page 122.

# Sound, vibration and gravity

Sounds are really vibrations in the air. In mammals, the sense organs for sound are the ears. Your ears also help you keep your balance.

**Animals with large ears, such as rabbits and bats, tend to be very sensitive to sound. Bats only come out at night, so they rely on hearing to detect their prey.**

**Fish don't have ears. They pick up vibrations by means of sensitive cells along a part of the body called the lateral line.**

**Animals with long whiskers, such as hamsters, are sensitive to vibrations.**

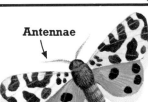

**Lateral line**

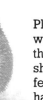

**Keep the soil well packed in.**

Plants are sensitive to gravity. No matter which way you plant a seed, it will grow in the right direction. Try turning a young shoot on its side. Leave it in the dark for a few days and keep it well watered. What happens? ▶

# Smell and taste

In mammals, the nose and tongue are the sense organs for smell and taste. Many animals have a much better sense of smell than humans. This helps them search for food and avoid being eaten.

**Antennae**

**Insects, such as moths, smell with their antennae.**

**Flies taste with their feet. They walk over their food before eating it.**

# Touch

The skin is the organ for sensing touch, pain and temperature. There are sensitive nerve endings all over your skin. Very sensitive parts, such as the tongue and fingertips, have more nerve endings.

The back has fewer nerves than other parts. Try touching a friend's back with the ends of two pencils, about 2cm apart. Ask how many pencils there are. Sometimes they may feel them as one touch.

# Sensitive plants

Some plants are sensitive to touch. If you touch a Mimosa pudica plant, the leaves will close suddenly and the plant will droop. This makes them less easy to eat.

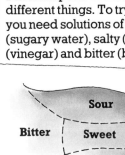

# Draw a map of your tongue

Different parts of the tongue can taste different things. To try this experiment, you need solutions of something sweet (sugary water), salty (salty water), sour (vinegar) and bitter (black tea).

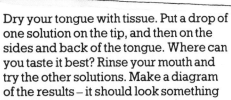

Dry your tongue with tissue. Put a drop of one solution on the tip, and then on the sides and back of the tongue. Where can you taste it best? Rinse your mouth and try the other solutions. Make a diagram of the results – it should look something like this.

121

# Co-ordination

All living things need some means of co-ordinating their activities, so that the different parts of their bodies work together as a whole. In most animals, this is achieved by some sort of nervous system. The nervous system in mammals consists of the brain and spinal cord, with bundles of fibres called nerves. Each fibre is part of a nerve cell, called a neurone. Nerves act rather like messengers. It is their job to send messages, in the form of nerve impulses, to and from different parts of the body.

## How it works

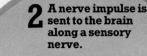

**1** You detect danger with one or more of your sense organs.

**2** A nerve impulse is sent to the brain along a sensory nerve.

**3** The brain interprets the message and decides what the response should be – in this case, to run.

**4** A nerve impulse is sent along a motor nerve to the muscles.

**5** The muscles receive the message. They contract, causing your body to move.

All this happens in fractions of a second.

## Insect nervous system

An insect's nervous system works in a similar way. Though instead of a brain, it has several organs called ganglia*, the largest of which is in its head. The ganglia receive messages from the sense organs and direct them to other parts of the body.

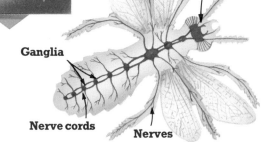

Large ganglion in head

Ganglia

Nerve cords

Nerves

Do you think sneezing or blinking are reflex reactions?

## Reflex actions

Many actions, such as kicking a ball, require a conscious decision from the brain. They are called voluntary reactions, because you choose to do them. But there are some actions which are automatic and can by-pass part of the brain. These are called involuntary, or reflex, reactions. Most reflex reactions happen to protect you. For instance, if you touch something hot, your hand will automatically leap away.

122

*The singular is ganglion.

# Keeping things under control

In order for the body to work properly, a lot of things have to be kept under control. For instance, the supply of water and the level of the various substances in the blood need to be regulated. Many of these processes, in plants as well as animals, are co-ordinated by chemicals called hormones. In animals, hormones are made by organs called endocrine glands and released into the blood. Hormones do a variety of jobs. For example, if you are excited or in danger, a hormone called adrenalin is produced. Here you can see what it does.

**Your heart beats faster and blood rushes to your muscles from other parts of the body. This gives you more power if you need to run or fight.**

**Your muscles generate heat, so you sweat more to get rid of the heat.**

**To give you more energy, you respire faster. This makes your breathing quicker.**

**If there is an accident, your blood will clot faster.**

**As blood has been diverted away from your skin and stomach, your skin goes pale and you get "butterflies" in the stomach.**

**Adrenalin makes the cells take up more oxygen and glucose, so they can work faster.**

## Temperature control

The temperature of the body needs to be kept steady. This is because enzymes, which are vital to many of the body's activities, can only function within a certain range of temperatures. There are various ways of controlling temperature.

When you become too hot, the blood vessels nearest the skin widen, so that more blood passes through them. This makes you look red. Heat from the blood passes through the skin into the air. ▶

Sweat is mainly water and salt. When you get too hot, it comes up through your pores and evaporates. This cools you down.

When you are too cold, your muscles try to compensate by increasing their activity, to create heat. This activity is shivering. ▶

Mammals and birds are called warm-blooded animals, because they can maintain a constant temperature. The activities in their bodies produce heat which they can retain by insulation – with fur, feathers or a layer of fat under the skin.

Cold-blooded animals, such as snakes, do not necessarily have cold blood. But they cannot create as much heat inside their bodies. They bask in summer, in order to absorb heat from the Sun.

**Penguins have a layer of fat under their skin, which helps them survive in cold climates.**

123

# Reproduction

All animals and plants die eventually. But they pass on their characteristics by reproducing themselves. Most organisms produce offspring from two parents, but some can reproduce from only one.

## What is sexual reproduction?

In sexual reproduction, a new animal or plant is formed from two parents. Most animals and flowering plants reproduce sexually. A male sex cell joins a female sex cell to make a single new cell called a zygote. The zygote divides many times, producing more cells which form the new individual. Sex cells are called gametes and are produced by sex organs. The fusing together of gametes is called fertilization.

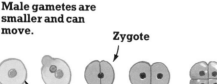

**Male gametes are smaller and can move.**

**Zygote**

**Female gametes are larger, but fewer of them are produced.**

**Gametes fusing to form a zygote.**

**The zygote grows to form an embryo.**

**Seed contains plant embryo**

**Animal embryo**

## Plant sex organs

A plant's sex organs are in its flowers. Some plants have male and female organs in the same flower; others have separate male and female flowers. The female sex organs are called carpels. Each carpel contains an ovary and each ovary contains one or more ovules. The female gametes, or eggs, are enclosed in the ovules. The male sex organs are called stamens. Each stamen consists of a stalk with an anther on the end.

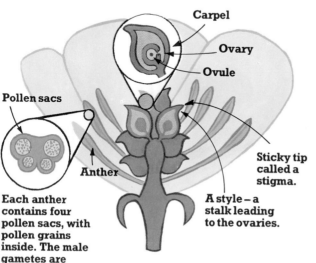

**Carpel**

**Ovary**

**Ovule**

**Pollen sacs**

**Anther**

**Each anther contains four pollen sacs, with pollen grains inside. The male gametes are contained in the pollen grains.**

**A style – a stalk leading to the ovaries.**

**Sticky tip called a stigma.**

## Animal sex organs

Animals' sex organs all have the same basic features. Here you can see human sex organs. A few animals have both male and female organs.

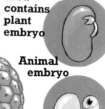

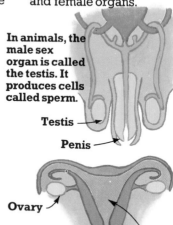

**In animals, the male sex organ is called the testis. It produces cells called sperm.**

**Testis**

**Penis**

**Ovary**

**The female sex organ is called the ovary. It produces cells called ova or eggs.**

**Uterus or womb**

You could try dissecting a large flower, such as a tulip, very carefully with a sharp kitchen knife. Use a magnifying glass to help you identify the different parts.

124

# How fertilization happens

Many animals that live in water, such as fish, produce large numbers of eggs and sperm. These are released into the water at the same time. The sperm, which have tails, swim towards the eggs to fertilize them. This is called external fertilization, as it takes place outside the parents' bodies. This method is very risky, as many eggs are eaten and sperm are lost.

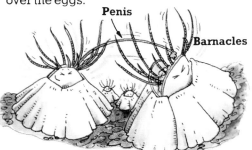
Sperm
Eggs

External fertilization would not work on land as the sperm could not swim to meet the eggs. Most land animals, including humans, (and many water animals) use internal fertilization, which is a more efficient method. The male deposits sperm inside the female's body by means of an organ called a penis.

Some animals, such as frogs, also practise external fertilization, but with a better chance of success. The male clings to the female's back until the eggs are released. Then he releases his sperm so that it pours over the eggs.

Penis

Barnacles

# Pollination

Before fertilization can take place in plants, pollen must be transferred from the anthers to a stigma. This is called pollination. Since flowers cannot move, they rely on one of two methods – animals (usually insects) or wind – to carry the pollen.

**Animal-pollinated flowers have brightly coloured, scented petals to attract the animal.**

**Insects feed on pollen and nectar.**

**Some flowers are pollinated by other animals, such as birds and bats.**

**Wind-pollinated flowers do not need to be colourful or scented.**

**They produce large quantities of pollen, as more tends to get lost.**

**The male flower has long, protruding anthers, well-exposed to the wind.**

**The female flowers often have large, feathery stigmas, which make an easy target to hit.**

## How it happens

The insect visits the flower in search of food. As it does so, it gets brushed with pollen which is picked up by the sticky stigmas of the next flower it visits.

## Fertilization

Pollen grain

Pollen tube

When the pollen lands it sends a tube down the style and into the ovary. Gametes move down the tube to fertilize the egg.

Ovary

125

## How the embryo develops

The embryos of frogs and fish develop inside soft eggs in the water. Many of them do not survive as they are often left to develop on their own.

Some land animals, such as birds and reptiles, produce eggs with a hard or leathery shell. This protects the embryo inside and stops it drying up.

### Finding somewhere to grow

A plant embryo is contained inside a seed. The seed has a hard, protective wall around it and a store of food inside. Seeds have a better chance of surviving if they grow away from the parent plants. This stops the ground becoming overcrowded. Seeds are designed so that they can be scattered in one of several ways.

The embryos of mammals develop inside the body of the mother. Mammals and birds both look after their offspring. So although they produce relatively small numbers, each one has a better chance of survival.

### By animals

The seeds are held by fruits. ▶
Some fruits, such as strawberries and tomatoes, are fleshy and attractive. Animals eat the fruits and the seeds pass through the animals' bodies.

◀ Not all fruits are edible. Some fruits have hooks on them which catch in the fur of passing animals.

### By wind

Seeds which are light and ▶ have wings or hairs, such as sycamore seeds, are scattered by the wind.

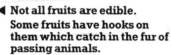

### By explosion

◀ Some seeds develop in pods and are scattered when the pod bursts open.

Which method do you think would take the seed furthest?

## How male seahorses give birth

A female seahorse's eggs are fertilized externally, then deposited in a pouch in the body of the male. As the eggs grow, his body swells in size. The eggs split open inside the pouch, but the young seahorses do not emerge until they are fully developed.

**Young seahorse**

# Asexual reproduction

In asexual reproduction, offspring are produced from one parent only. This method is used mainly by the simplest organisms, such as bacteria, and by plants that don't have flowers. But many flowering plants, and some animals, have asexual as well as sexual methods.

## Cell division

Dividing in two is the most frequent method of reproduction in single-celled organisms, such as amoebae* and many bacteria. The nucleus splits and cytoplasm gathers around each one, forming two identical cells.

Some bacteria can divide as often as once every 20 minutes. Can you work out how many bacteria could be produced from one in 10 hours?

## Spores

Many non-flowering plants, such as fungi, produce tiny cells called spores. These are scattered by rain, wind or insects, and develop into a new individual. If you see a mature puff ball, you could try dropping water on it. It may shed its spores.

## Budding

Hydras are tiny animals, about 2cm long, that live in ponds and slow-moving streams. They can reproduce by budding – growing a new animal on the sides of their bodies.

## Asexual reproduction in flowering plants

All flowering plants reproduce sexually by means of seeds, but many of them have asexual methods too.

### Runners ▶

Some plants, such as spider plants, put down runners. These are long side shoots which touch the ground and develop roots of their own.

**Parent plant** **New plants** **Runners**

### ◀ Tubers

A potato is a swollen stem, called a tuber. It develops from shoots of a potato plant, which grow into the soil instead of producing branches. Food is stored in the tuber. In winter the plant dies, but the tubers develop into new plants in the following year.

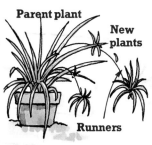

**Potato plant** **Potato tubers**

### Single parents

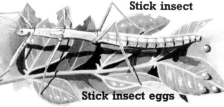

**Stick insect**

**Stick insect eggs ▼**

Nearly all stick insects are females. So they produce young from eggs which have not been fertilized. This is called parthenogenesis, which comes from the Greek, meaning "virgin births". Other insects, such as aphids (greenfly), also reproduce by parthenogenesis.

### Bulbs ▶

A bulb is a bud whose leaves are swollen with food. It stays alive over winter when the rest of the plant has died. Sometimes the bulb reproduces asexually, by sprouting an extra bulb to one side.

**New bulb** **Main bulb**

127

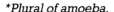

*Plural of amoeba.

# Life cycles and growth

Most animals and plants begin life as a single cell. The cell divides many times, adding to itself new cells, and so the organism increases in size. As it does so, its structure becomes more complicated, and it develops specialized cells for particular jobs. Some organisms, such as trees, go on growing all their lives. Others, like us, reach a certain size and then stop. The changes that an organism undergoes in the course of its life is known as its life cycle.

## Investigating seeds

The life cycle of a plant starts with a seed. You could try investigating the structure of a seed. Soak some large seeds, such as broad bean seeds, in water overnight. The water makes them swell and easy to split open. You should be able to see a tiny embryo growing inside.

## Growing seeds

In order to germinate, or develop into a plant, a seed needs water, oxygen and a reasonable temperature (not below freezing point). Seeds can germinate without soil. You could try growing some cress on damp blotting paper or cotton wool.

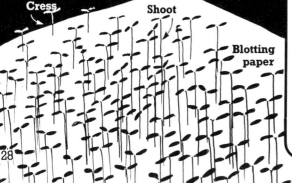

Cress  Shoot  Blotting paper

## Plant life cycles

The life cycles of many plants are adapted to suit their climates and surroundings. Winters, or dry periods, can be tough on plants, so they have ways of becoming dormant. They stop feeding and growing and all their activities are slowed down until spring.

## Annuals

Many garden flowers are annuals. This means that they live for one year only, growing and flowering in the warm period. In winter the leaves and flowers die, but the seeds remain to grow into new plants.

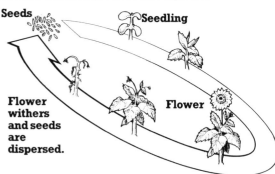

Seeds  Seedling

Flower withers and seeds are dispersed.  Flower

Seeds are well-adapted to survive winter. Their hard coat keeps out the cold. Their food store keeps them alive until spring, when they can produce leaves of their own and start carrying out photosynthesis.

## Perennials

Trees and shrubs, such as roses, are perennials. They live for many years, as well as making seeds for new plants. In winter many become dormant. Their leaves drop off, which stops them losing water by transpiration. This means they can't carry out photosynthesis, so they live on stores of food in the stem and roots.

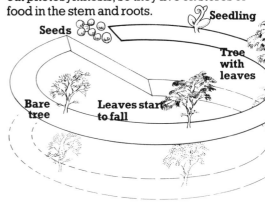

Seeds  Seedling

Tree with leaves

Bare tree  Leaves start to fall

# Some animal life cycles

Some animals, such as insects and frogs, change their form several times in the course of their life cycle. This is called metamorphosis. These different stages can help the animal by providing a form in which it can survive the winter. The animal often feeds on different foods at different stages, which helps avoid competition for food between parents and young.

## Butterfly's life cycle

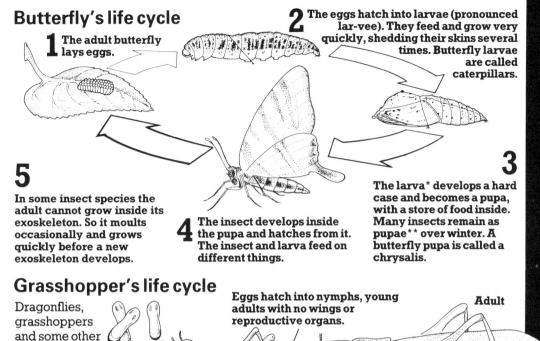

**1** The adult butterfly lays eggs.

**2** The eggs hatch into larvae (pronounced lar-vee). They feed and grow very quickly, shedding their skins several times. Butterfly larvae are called caterpillars.

**3** The larva* develops a hard case and becomes a pupa, with a store of food inside. Many insects remain as pupae** over winter. A butterfly pupa is called a chrysalis.

**4** The insect develops inside the pupa and hatches from it. The insect and larva feed on different things.

**5** In some insect species the adult cannot grow inside its exoskeleton. So it moults occasionally and grows quickly before a new exoskeleton develops.

## Grasshopper's life cycle

Dragonflies, grasshoppers and some other insects, have only three stages in their life cycle.

**Eggs**

Eggs hatch into nymphs, young adults with no wings or reproductive organs.

**Adult**

## Frog's life cycle

A frog is another animal that undergoes metamorphosis. It takes about four months from egg to frog.

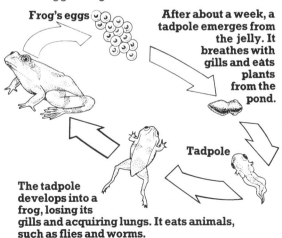

**Frog's eggs**

After about a week, a tadpole emerges from the jelly. It breathes with gills and eats plants from the pond.

**Tadpole**

The tadpole develops into a frog, losing its gills and acquiring lungs. It eats animals, such as flies and worms.

## Watch a fly's life cycle

If you want to study the life cycle of a fly, you could capture some flies and leave them in a jar with some meat.

A complete cycle can take only 21 days.

Muslin lid, or tin with holes for breathing.

Meat for eggs to be laid on and for larvae to eat.

Sugar and food scraps for flies to eat.

*The singular of larvae.
**Pronounced pew-pee, the plural of pupa.

# Genetics and heredity

What makes you take after your parents? Some of the similarities may be due to your upbringing and environment, but many others, such as the colour of your eyes, are inherited. Characteristics like these are controlled by instructions called genes. The study of genes, and the rules that decide which features you inherit from which parent, is called genetics.

## Where are your genes?

Genes are spread out along thin, thread-like structures called chromosomes, which are in the nucleus of every cell. Chromosomes come in pairs. The number of pairs depends on the organism. Some plants have over 100 pairs of chromosomes in every cell; one species of worm has only one. Human beings have 23 pairs (or 46 chromosomes) in each cell.

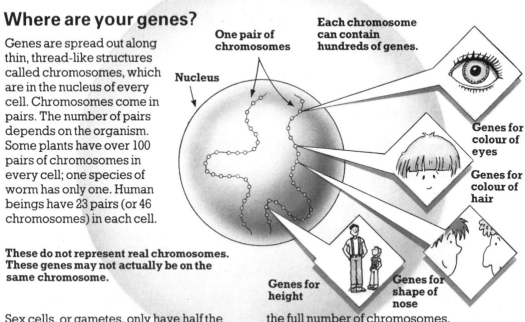

**One pair of chromosomes**

**Nucleus**

**Each chromosome can contain hundreds of genes.**

**Genes for colour of eyes**

**Genes for colour of hair**

**Genes for height**

**Genes for shape of nose**

**These do not represent real chromosomes. These genes may not actually be on the same chromosome.**

Sex cells, or gametes, only have half the usual number of chromosomes. When gametes fuse, they produce a zygote with the full number of chromosomes. Chromosomes come in pairs because you inherit one from each parent.

## How sex is determined

Of the 46 chromosomes in human cells, two are sex chromosomes. They can be of two kinds, X and Y. Females have two X chromosomes, males have an X and a Y.

**A gamete, or egg, from a female has 22 ordinary chromosomes and one X.**

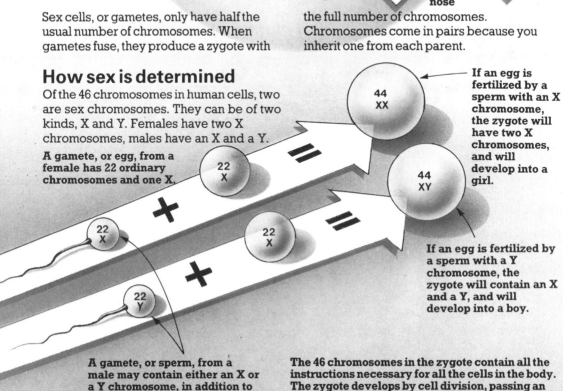

44
XX

22
X

22
X

22
X

44
XY

22
Y

**If an egg is fertilized by a sperm with an X chromosome, the zygote will have two X chromosomes, and will develop into a girl.**

**If an egg is fertilized by a sperm with a Y chromosome, the zygote will contain an X and a Y, and will develop into a boy.**

**A gamete, or sperm, from a male may contain either an X or a Y chromosome, in addition to the 22 other ones.**

**The 46 chromosomes in the zygote contain all the instructions necessary for all the cells in the body. The zygote develops by cell division, passing an exact copy of these instructions to each new cell.**

# What are genes made of?

Genes are composed of sections of the chemical DNA (deoxyribonucleic acid), which controls the activities in all living cells. Its structure was first discovered in Cambridge in 1953, by James Watson and Francis Crick.

**Each molecule\* of DNA is shaped in a double helix – like two spiral staircases wound round each other.**

**DNA carries its genes, or instructions, in a sort of code. The arrangement of chemicals along the spiral varies according to the instructions being coded.**

**Each step in the spiral consists of one of these two pairs.**

**DNA contains four chemicals linked in pairs – adenine and thymine, cytosine and guanine.**

## How genes were discovered

The idea of genes, or factors, as he called them, was first worked out in 1865 by Gregor Mendel, a Czech monk. He experimented with breeding pea plants, working out how characteristics such as height and colour were inherited.

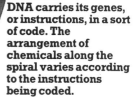

## Dominant and recessive genes

Your cells contain at least two genes for each characteristic – one from each parent – but these are very often in conflict with one another. For instance, you might inherit a gene for brown eyes from your mother, and one for blue eyes from your father. What determines what your eye colour will be? Mendel solved this by discovering that one gene is often hidden by the other. The hidden gene is called "recessive", and the one that hides it is called "dominant".

**In sweet peas, white is a recessive colour and red is a dominant one. Biologists show this by writing a capital "R" for red and a small letter "r" for white.**

**If you breed from a red and a white plant, the new plants will all be red. But they will each have one R (red) and one r (white) gene.**

**If you breed from two plants with Rr genes, their offspring will probably be in a ratio of three red to one white. Follow this diagram to see why.**

**To have recessive characteristics, offspring must receive a recessive gene from both parents.**

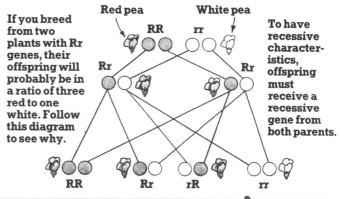

Red pea — RR    White pea — rr

Rr            Rr

RR    Rr    rR    rr

## Genetic puzzle

Try to work out what will happen if you mate a spotted rabbit, with two dominant genes (SS), with a black rabbit, with two recessive genes (ss). What colour will their offspring be? And if one of them were mated with a rabbit with identical genes, what colour, or colours, would their offspring be?

*A molecule is the smallest part of a substance that can normally exist by itself.*

## Organizing biology

In order to make biology easier to study, biologists divide living organisms into groups with similar characteristics. They use the system of classification drawn up in the 18th century by the Swedish botanist, Karl von Linne. Living organisms are first divided into the animal and plant kingdoms*. Each animal and plant belongs to a species and has a species name, which consists of two words in Latin. A species is a group of organisms that are similar to each other and can breed together. Humans are one species; dogs are another. Each species belongs to a series of larger groups, as you can see in the chart below. A phylum is a main group and a class is a sub-group.

KINGDOM

PHYLUM

CLASS

ORDER

FAMILY

GENUS

SPECIES

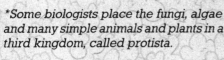

*Some biologists place the fungi, algae and many simple animals and plants in a third kingdom, called protista.

# The plant kingdom

Here you can find out about the main groups and classes in the plant kingdom.

## 1 Algae

Algae are very simple plants with no stems, roots or leaves. They grow in very wet or damp places. Seaweed and pondweed are types of algae.

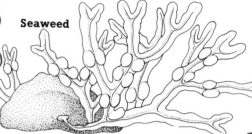

**Seaweed**

Look out for green slime on the surface of ponds. This is probably spirogyra, an algae made up of lots of single cells held together in threads.

## 7 Flowering plants

Flowering plants are also seed-bearing plants. They include trees as well as flowers. Their seeds are produced inside a fruit, which develops from a flower. Flowering plants are the most advanced, complex kind of plant.

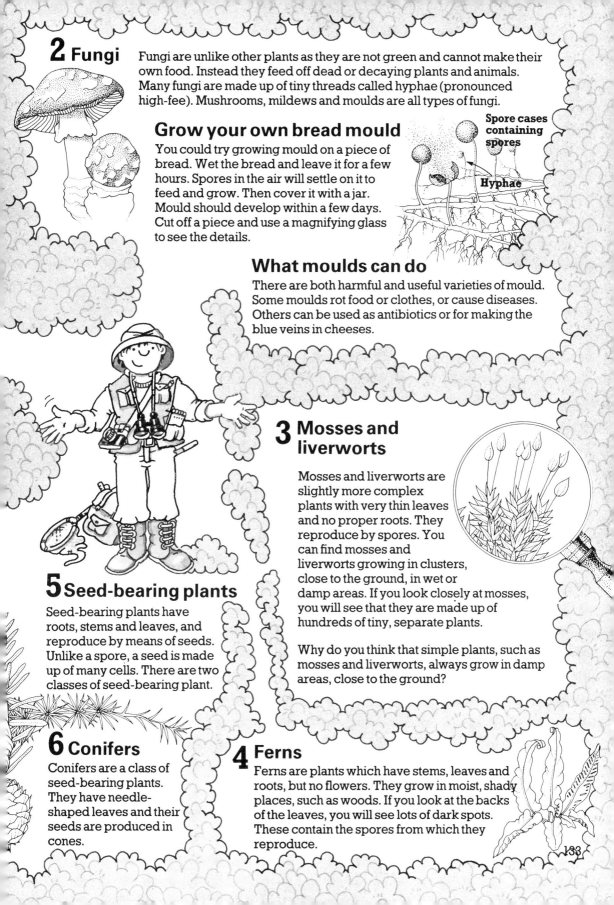

## 2 Fungi

Fungi are unlike other plants as they are not green and cannot make their own food. Instead they feed off dead or decaying plants and animals. Many fungi are made up of tiny threads called hyphae (pronounced high-fee). Mushrooms, mildews and moulds are all types of fungi.

### Grow your own bread mould

You could try growing mould on a piece of bread. Wet the bread and leave it for a few hours. Spores in the air will settle on it to feed and grow. Then cover it with a jar. Mould should develop within a few days. Cut off a piece and use a magnifying glass to see the details.

**Spore cases containing spores**

**Hyphae**

### What moulds can do

There are both harmful and useful varieties of mould. Some moulds rot food or clothes, or cause diseases. Others can be used as antibiotics or for making the blue veins in cheeses.

## 3 Mosses and liverworts

Mosses and liverworts are slightly more complex plants with very thin leaves and no proper roots. They reproduce by spores. You can find mosses and liverworts growing in clusters, close to the ground, in wet or damp areas. If you look closely at mosses, you will see that they are made up of hundreds of tiny, separate plants.

Why do you think that simple plants, such as mosses and liverworts, always grow in damp areas, close to the ground?

## 5 Seed-bearing plants

Seed-bearing plants have roots, stems and leaves, and reproduce by means of seeds. Unlike a spore, a seed is made up of many cells. There are two classes of seed-bearing plant.

## 6 Conifers

Conifers are a class of seed-bearing plants. They have needle-shaped leaves and their seeds are produced in cones.

## 4 Ferns

Ferns are plants which have stems, leaves and roots, but no flowers. They grow in moist, shady places, such as woods. If you look at the backs of the leaves, you will see lots of dark spots. These contain the spores from which they reproduce.

133

# The animal kingdom

In this section you can find out about some of the main classes and phyla of the animal kingdom. Mammals, birds, fish, reptiles and amphibians are all vertebrates. The simplest animals are called invertebrates, which means that they have no solid internal skeleton.

You may be able to find a variety of invertebrates to study just by looking in a garden or a park. You could try to find out what species they belong to, what they eat, what living conditions they like, when they are active (day or night) and how they move.

## Protozoa

One-celled animals, such as amoebae, belong to the protozoa phylum. Protozoa usually live in water – in the sea, in ponds or in damp places, such as puddles – but you need a microscope to be able to see them.

## Coelenterates

Coelenterates (pronounced see-lenterates) are animals with soft, hollow bodies and tentacles. Jellyfish, sea anemones and corals are all coelenterates.

## Annelids

Garden worms belong to a phylum called annelids. They have soft bodies, divided into rings or segments. Worms move by relaxing and contracting muscles in their bodies.

## Arthropods

Arthropods have an exoskeleton, jointed legs and antennae. Their bodies are usually divided into three sections – head, thorax and abdomen. There are four main classes of arthropod.

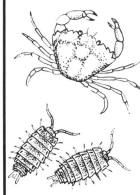

### Crustaceans

Woodlice and shellfish, such as crabs and prawns are crustacea. They have between 10 and 14 legs, two pairs of antennae, and they respire by means of gills.

### Arachnids

Spiders and scorpions are arachnids. They have eight legs, no antennae, and simple rather than compound eyes. Some arachnids spin webs for trapping their food.

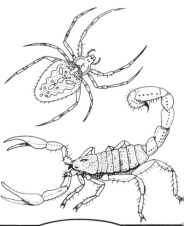

## Molluscs

Molluscs are soft-bodied animals with shells and a single foot. Snails, slugs and mussels are all molluscs.

If you find a snail, you could mark its shell with paint, and put it back outside. Then you could watch its movements to find out what kind of habitat it likes or how far it travels in a day.

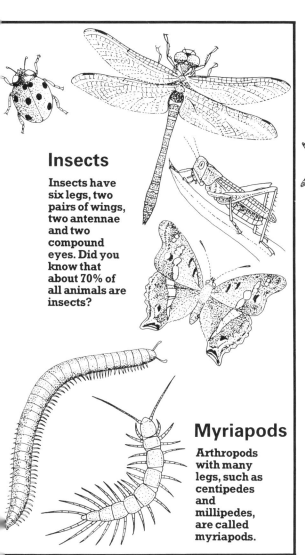

## Insects

Insects have six legs, two pairs of wings, two antennae and two compound eyes. Did you know that about 70% of all animals are insects?

## Myriapods

Arthropods with many legs, such as centipedes and millipedes, are called myriapods.

## Vertebrates

All animals with a backbone are called vertebrates.

## Fish

**Fish are cold-blooded vertebrates. They have scales and fins, breathe with gills and live in water.**

## Amphibians

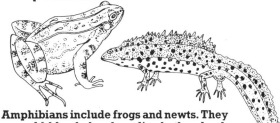

**Amphibians include frogs and newts. They are cold-blooded and can live both on land and in water. They lay eggs in water.**

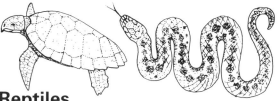

## Reptiles

**Reptiles include snakes, lizards and turtles. They have scaly skin and lay eggs with shells on land.**

## Birds

**Birds have feathers and wings and reproduce by laying eggs.**

## Mammals

**Mammals are warm-blooded vertebrates with hair. They have lungs and two pairs of limbs and they feed their young with milk.**

## Echinoderms

Echinoderms are spiny-skinned animals, such as starfish and sea urchins.

135

# Classification computer program

If you have a microcomputer, or can borrow one, you could use this program to help you classify an animal. Think of an animal, then answer the questions to find out which phylum it belongs to. In some cases you can find out its class and order too. The program is written to work on a Commodore 64 or VIC 20 microcomputer. Lines that need changing for other computers are marked with a symbol and printed at the end of the program. Each symbol corresponds to a different computer. They are:

▲ **BBC**          ■ **ZX SPECTRUM**          ● **APPLE**

```
 10 GOSUB 380
 20 LET N=1
 30 GOSUB 320
 40 IF N<=NQ THEN GOSUB 140:GOTO 60
 50 IF N>100 THEN GOSUB 210
 60 IF N=999 THEN GOTO 120
 70 IF N<>0 THEN GOTO 40
 80 PRINT:PRINT "DO YOU WANT TO CLASSIFY ANOTHER ANIMAL"
 90 PRINT:GOSUB 300
100 IF A$="Y" THEN GOTO 20
110 PRINT "BYE...":STOP
120 PRINT:PRINT "SORRY - WE CANNOT CLASSIFY YOUR ANIMAL"
130 GOTO 80
140 GOSUB 280
150 PRINT B$(S(N));" ";
160 RESTORE:FOR I=1 TO N:READ M$:NEXT I
170 PRINT M$:PRINT:PRINT:GOSUB 300
180 IF A$="Y" THEN LET N=Y(N)
190 IF A$="N" THEN LET N=N(N)
200 RETURN
210 GOSUB 280:GOSUB 360
220 FOR I=1 TO N-100:READ M$:NEXT I
230 PRINT "YOU HAVE A MEMBER OF THE ";M$
240 LET N=L(N-100):GOSUB 260:RETURN
250 GOSUB 260:RETURN
260 PRINT:PRINT "PRESS RETURN TO CONTINUE"
270 INPUT A$:RETURN
280 PRINT CHR$(147)
290 RETURN
300 PRINT "ANSWER Y/N"
310 INPUT A$:RETURN
320 GOSUB 280:PRINT "THINK OF AN ANIMAL":PRINT
330 PRINT "ANSWER THESE QUESTIONS TO"
340 PRINT "CLASSIFY IT"
350 GOSUB 260:RETURN
360 RESTORE:FOR I=1 TO NQ:READ M$
370 NEXT I:RETURN
380 LET NQ=19:LET NS=19:GOSUB 360
390 DIM Y(NQ):DIM N(NQ):DIM L(NS):DIM S(NQ):DIM B$(4)
400 FOR I=1 TO NS:READ M$:NEXT I
```

## How to adapt the program

This is a very simple program, but it will give you an idea of how biologists can use computers to help them classify living things. The program has been written so that you can adapt it if you want to. You can expand the program by including extra questions and statements to classify an animal in more detail.

To ask another question, look at line 3200. Which of these phrases does your question begin with? Insert a number at the end of line 3210. If the question begins with "Does it have", insert 1, if it begins with "Is it", insert 2, and so on. After line 1180, add a new line – 1190 – and the rest of your question. After line 2090, add line 2100 and your answer. If there are no further questions, add a 0 at the end of line 3100. If you want to ask a further question, insert the number of that question – probably 21. (There are 19 questions in the program as it stands.) You also need to adjust line 380. NQ stands for the number of questions in the program, and NS for the number of statements or answers.

```
      410 FOR I=1 TO NQ:READ Y(I):READ N(I):NEXT I
      420 FOR I=1 TO NS:READ L(I):NEXT I
      430 FOR I=1 TO 4:READ B$(I):NEXT I
      440 FOR I=1 TO NQ:READ S(I):NEXT I
      450 RETURN

1000 DATA "A SOLID INTERNAL SKELETON"
1010 DATA "MADE ONLY OF ONE CELL"
1020 DATA "IN WATER AND HAVE STINGING TENTACLES"
1030 DATA "A SOFT BODY, DIVIDED INTO RINGS OR SEGMENTS"
1040 DATA "AN EXTERNAL SKELETON"
1050 DATA "TWO PAIRS OF ANTENNAE AND BETWEEN 10 AND 14 LEGS"
1060 DATA "8 LEGS AND NO ANTENNAE"
1070 DATA "6 LEGS AND 3 BODY SECTIONS"
1080 DATA "A LONG BODY AND MANY LEGS"
1090 DATA "A SOFT BODY ENCLOSED IN A SHELL"
1100 DATA "IN THE SEA AND HAVE A SPINY SKIN"
1110 DATA "IN WATER, HAVE SCALES AND BREATHE WITH GILLS"
1120 DATA "MOIST SKIN, LIVE ON LAND, BUT LAY ITS EGGS IN WATER"
1130 DATA "ON LAND, HAVE SCALY SKIN AND LAY EGGS WITH SHELLS"
1140 DATA "WINGS WITH FEATHERS"
1150 DATA "WARM BLOODED AND DOES IT SUCKLE ITS YOUNG WITH MILK"
1160 DATA "LAY EGGS"
1170 DATA "A POUCH"
1180 DATA "YOUNG WHICH DEVELOP INSIDE A PLACENTA"

2000 DATA "VERTEBRATE SUBPHYLUM (CHORDATA PHYLUM)"
2010 DATA "PHYLUM PROTOZOA","PHYLUM COELENTERATES"
2020 DATA "PHYLUM ANNELIDS","PHYLUM ARTHROPOD"
2030 DATA "CLASS CRUSTACEA","CLASS ARACHNIDS"
2040 DATA "CLASS INSECTS","MYRIAPOD CLASS"
2050 DATA "MOLLUSC PHYLUM","PHYLUM ECHINODERM"
2060 DATA "FISH CLASS","AMPHIBIAN CLASS"
2070 DATA "CLASS REPTILES","CLASS BIRDS"
2080 DATA "CLASS MAMMALS","MONOTREME FAMILY"
2090 DATA "MARSUPIAL FAMILY","EUTHERIAN FAMILY"

3000 DATA 101,2,102,3,103,4,104,5,105,10,106,7,107,8,108,9,109,999
3010 DATA 110,11,111,999,112,13,113,14,114,15,115,16,116,999
3020 DATA 117,18,118,19,119,999
3100 DATA 12,0,0,0,6,0,0,0,0,0,0,0,0,0,0,0,17,0,0,0
3200 DATA "DOES IT HAVE","IS IT","DOES IT LIVE","DOES IT"
3210 DATA 1,2,3,1,1,1,1,1,1,1,1,3,3,1,3,1,2,4,1,1
```

Below is a list of changes that will enable you to run this program on other computers too. These instructions need to be inserted into program in the relevant places.

■ 150 LET C$=B$(S(N))

■ 152 IF C$(LEN(C$))=" " THEN LET C$=C$
( TO LEN(C$)-1):GOTO 152

■ 155 PRINT C$;" ";

● 280 HOME

▲ ■ 280 CLS:PRINT:PRINT

■ 390 Change DIM B$(4) to DIM B$(4,12)

# Ecology and the environment

Ecology is the study of the relationship between animals and plants and their surroundings. A group of animals and plants that live together are known as a community. The place where they live is called their habitat. Sometimes a living organism, such as a tree, provides a habitat for other plants and animals. The organisms in a habitat compete with each other for survival. They also depend on each other in many ways, for feeding or reproducing. Biologists refer to a community and its habitat as an ecosystem.

**Insects and birds make nests in the branches.**

**Caterpillars feed on the leaves.**

A tree is a habitat. This one is in a tropical forest.

**Plants, such as ferns, mosses and orchids, put down roots in the bark, or use the trunk as a means of support.**

You could make a study of the plants and animals in a large tree.

## Competing for light

Organisms can co-exist successfully if they don't have to compete with each other. For instance, in a wood most of the light is captured by the tallest trees. However some plants, such as bluebells, grow and flower in the spring, while the trees are still bare. By the time the trees are green, these plants have withered.

You could investigate the different plants competing with each other on a lawn. Grass can shield other plants by growing taller.

But in areas that are well trampled, plants with wide leaves, such as daisies, can stunt grass seedlings.

## Living together

Some plants and animals depend on each other in very specific ways. If the relationship benefits both of them, it is called symbiosis. If it only benefits one of them, it is called commensalism. If the relationship harms one of the partners, it is called parasitism.

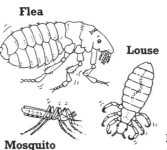

**Flea**

**Louse**

**Mosquito**

Lice, mosquitoes and fleas are all parasites. They get their food from the living bodies of other animals.

Sea anemones sometimes travel on the backs of hermit crabs. The crab is protected from attackers by the anemone's stinging tentacles. The anemone eats scraps of food left over by the crab.

**Sea anemone**

**Hermit crab**

# Food webs and chains

The animals and plants in a community are linked together into a complex food web. Increases in population are limited by the amount of food available, and by the fact that many organisms are eaten or die from disease. However, communities can change. If for some reason one species in a food web is wiped out, the rest of the web will be affected.

The organisms at the bottom of a food web are always more numerous than at the top. This is because the amount of energy passed along is reduced with each link in the chain. So biologists sometimes organize ecosystems into pyramids of feeding levels.

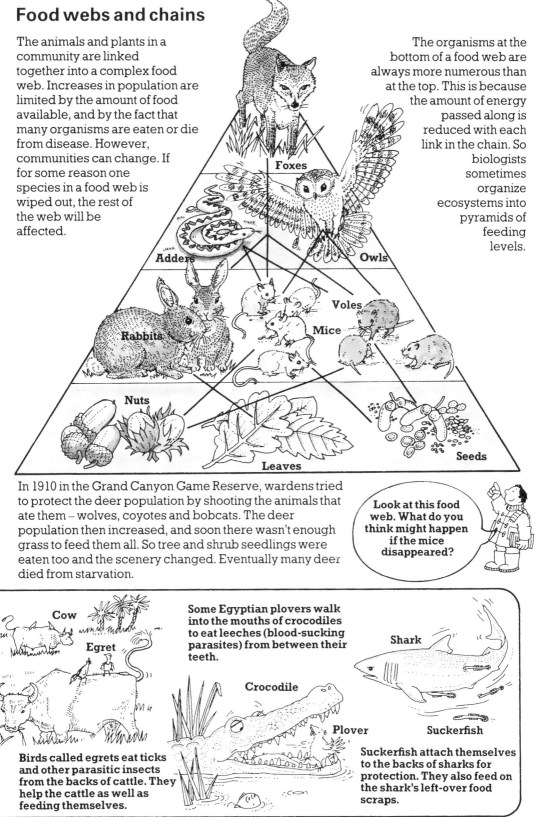

Foxes

Adders

Owls

Rabbits

Voles

Mice

Nuts

Leaves

Seeds

In 1910 in the Grand Canyon Game Reserve, wardens tried to protect the deer population by shooting the animals that ate them – wolves, coyotes and bobcats. The deer population then increased, and soon there wasn't enough grass to feed them all. So tree and shrub seedlings were eaten too and the scenery changed. Eventually many deer died from starvation.

Look at this food web. What do you think might happen if the mice disappeared?

Cow

Egret

Some Egyptian plovers walk into the mouths of crocodiles to eat leeches (blood-sucking parasites) from between their teeth.

Shark

Crocodile

Plover

Suckerfish

Birds called egrets eat ticks and other parasitic insects from the backs of cattle. They help the cattle as well as feeding themselves.

Suckerfish attach themselves to the backs of sharks for protection. They also feed on the shark's left-over food scraps.

139

## What is pollution?

Pollution is the release of substances into the air, water or soil, which may kill or harm living organisms. There are many sources of pollution. Factories produce poisonous waste products which are released into the air as smoke, or flow into rivers and streams. Car exhausts also give off poisonous gases, and sewage can cause damage if it is dumped in rivers.

## How rivers die

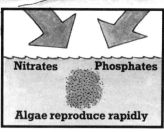

Nitrates    Phosphates

**Algae reproduce rapidly**

River with hardly any oxygen

Look out for green slime on the surface of rivers. This is made up of microscopic algae and is often a sign that a river is polluted.

Sewage, detergents and fertilizers all contain nitrates and phosphates which algae feed on. If these get into rivers, the algae reproduce rapidly.

When algae die, their bodies are broken down by bacteria. This process uses up oxygen. If the water loses a lot of oxygen, animals suffocate and die.

## Lichen test

You can find lichens* on the barks of trees, walls and other surfaces. They are very sensitive to pollution, so you can use them as a rough guide to how polluted your area is. In very polluted areas, there are no lichens. The cleaner the air, the greater the variety of lichens.

Shrubby lichens

Grey, leafy lichens

Yellow-orange leafy lichens

Grey-green crusty lichens

No lichens. Only pleurococcus, a green, powdery alga.

Clean air    Increasing pollution    Most pollution

### Acid test

You could try testing the acidity of the water in a local pond or stream. Use universal indicator papers. If the indicator number is less than 5, the water is unusually acid and may be polluted.

## How people affect the environment

Humans can alter the environment in many ways. Cutting down forests, to make way for cities and farms, destroys the natural habitat of many organisms. So animals and plants have to compete for less and less territory. Pesticides, which farmers use to protect their crops, can upset food chains by destroying links in them. Hunting for food, clothing or cosmetic products has led to the extinction of many species.

140

*Lichens are produced by an alga and a fungus living together.
**You can buy these at a chemist's.

# Competing for survival

Animals and plants produce large numbers of offspring, many of which are eaten or die before they reach maturity. Individuals within a species are never exactly alike, because of genetic differences. The ones that do survive tend to be stronger or better adapted for conditions in their environment. These characteristics are passed on, in their genes, to the next generation. In time, the characteristics of the unsuccessful individuals may die out. Biologists call this natural selection, or "survival of the fittest".

## Which ones survive?

If an animal or plant is better camouflaged than other members of its species, it is less likely to be seen and eaten. ▼

▲ Many animals, such as deer, compete in order to mate. The strongest male wins and usually mates with all the females in the herd.

Those that are more resistant to disease or can run away from predators are also more likely to survive. ▼

## Mutations

Sometimes, when a gamete is produced, a gene or chromosome is not copied properly. This leads to a variation, or mutation, in the instructions which produce the offspring. Most mutations are harmful. For instance, haemophilia (excessive bleeding because of a failure of the blood to clot) is the result of a mutation. However, if a mutation is beneficial, those individuals may survive to reproduce and may eventually outnumber the original variety.

Natural selection works very fast with bacteria, because they reproduce so rapidly. When a drug, such as penicillin, is used to kill bacteria, there are always a few immune bacteria which survive. These reproduce and the next generation of bacteria inherits immunity and so the drug becomes useless.

## The case of the peppered moth

Peppered moths are usually pale and speckled and hide on lichens. There is also a black variety, which until the industrial revolution in about 1850, was extremely rare in Britain. Then smoke from factories blackened the trees and killed the lichens, so the pale moths were no longer so well camouflaged. By 1895, black moths had increased to 98% of the population in industrial areas.

## Artificial selection

Farmers can use a knowledge of genetics to improve their crops and animals. For instance there might be a cow that produced a lot of milk but had a low resistance to disease, and another variety that was resistant to disease, but didn't produce much milk. Provided that the beneficial characteristics were controlled by dominant genes, a new and better type of cow could be produced by breeding from the two varieties.

# Using a microscope

If you've got a microscope, you could use it to investigate different parts of animals and plants. With most ordinary home microscopes, you can magnify things to about 400 times their size (×400). The field ion or electron microscopes that some scientists use can get a magnification of about ×1,000,000. An ordinary magnifying glass will magnify things to about 10 times their size. Here are some ideas for things you could look at and equipment that you will need.

Scalpel for cutting thin slices from specimens. If you haven't got one, you could use a razor blade, but be extremely careful not to cut yourself.

Bread board or old tile for cutting on.

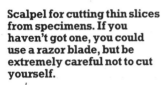

Stains are used to help you see the different parts of a specimen more clearly. Some parts absorb more of a stain than others. You could use iodine or kitchen food dyes.

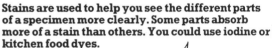

Tweezers for picking up delicate specimens.

Dropper for applying liquid.

## Looking at cells

You can get a sample of cheek cells by scraping the inside of your cheek with a finger. Put the liquid on a slide and add a drop of stain.

Cheek cells

To look at plant cells, you could mount a moss leaf in water. You should be able to see the cells and the green pigment inside the chloroplasts.

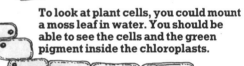

Moss cells

## Grow a pollen tube

Collect some pollen and mount it on a slide with a drop of sugar solution. (Add a teaspoonful of sugar to half a cup of water.) After about an hour, look to see if the pollen has germinated and grown a tube*.

Pollen grain

Pollen tube

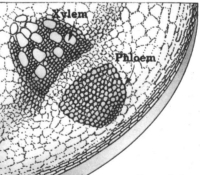

Xylem

Phloem

Petals

## Looking at xylem tubes

If you cut a thin slice off a stem, you could investigate the xylem vessels. Leave the stem in coloured water first**, so that the xylem shows up clearly. Mount the slice in water.

## Looking at stomata

If you coat a leaf with nail varnish, then peel the varnish off when it's dry, you will get a copy of the surface of the leaf. If you put this under the microscope, you should be able to see the shape of the stomata.

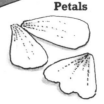

## Looking for colour

You could try to find out where the colour is located in petals, or in coloured stems, such as rhubarb. Is the cytoplasm coloured, or is the colour contained in structures like chloroplasts?

142

*This is not always successful. If it doesn't work, you could try solutions of different strengths. **See the experiment on page 116.

## Microscopic organisms

Pondwater contains numbers of microscopic organisms, such as amoebae. You could collect a bucket of pondwater and try a few drops at a time under the microscope. Here are a few of the organisms that you might see.

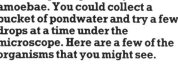

Vorticella

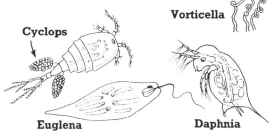

Cyclops

Euglena

Daphnia

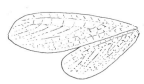

## Looking at insects

If you find dead insects, or other invertebrates, you could look at parts of their bodies, such as wings.

# Answers to puzzles

## Page 103: Why isn't a car a living thing?

A car isn't a living thing because it cannot grow or reproduce itself.

## Page 105

Fungi are plants that do not contain chlorophyll. Most other plants contain chlorophyll even if they are not green.

Some sea animals, such as sponges and barnacles, are not capable of locomotion when they are adults, although they can move when they are very young.

## Page 109: Monkey puzzle

Tree-living animals, such as monkeys, have forward-pointing eyes to help them judge distances accurately, as they jump from tree to tree.

## Page 112

When you do a lot of exercise, you use up extra energy. To get this energy your cells respire faster and use up oxygen more quickly. You pant in order to take in extra oxygen to compensate for this.

## Page 115

Your heart beats faster during exercise in order to speed up the flow of oxygen and food to the cells. This gives the cells more energy, so that your body can work harder.

## Page 116

Cacti have narrow spines as leaves in order to reduce the surface area from which water may be lost. Cacti live in dry places, such as deserts, where water is scarce.

Trees lose their leaves in winter to avoid losing too much water by transpiration. If the ground is frozen, it may be difficult for the roots to take in water.

## Page 122

Sneezing and blinking are both reflex actions.

## Page 127

If a bacteria divided once every 20 minutes, after 10 hours there would be 905,969,664 bacteria. Bacteria do not actually increase at this rate, because many are eaten or do not survive.

## Page 131: Genetics puzzle

If a black rabbit with two recessive black genes were mated with a spotted rabbit with two dominant spotted genes, all their offspring would be spotted. Each of the offspring would be spotted and would have one black gene and one spotted gene. If two rabbits of this kind were mated, they would produce three spotted rabbits for every one black one.

## Page 133

Many simple plants grow in damp areas close to the ground because they don't have proper root and stem systems. This means that they cannot efficiently transport water and other substances through their bodies.

## Page 139

If all the mice disappeared, the numbers of owls might decrease because of food shortages. Rival animals, like voles, might increase because their would be no competition from the mice.

# Index